Daddy's Shifter

Daddy's Shifter

Christine Barker

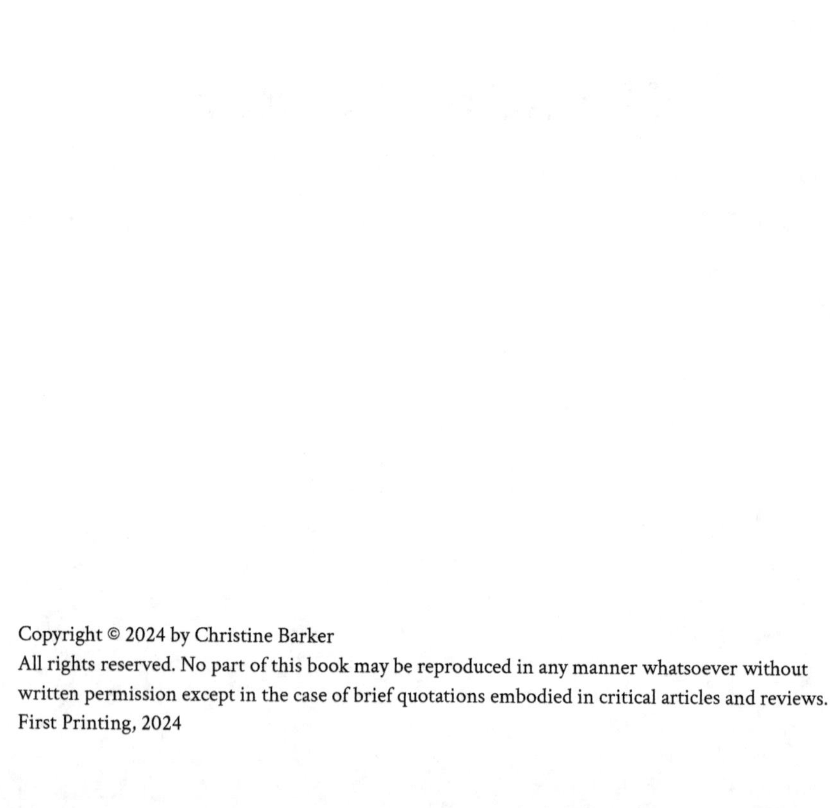

Contents

To the one who made me who I am today.

-Charmaine Harding

Prologue

Come little children to the shifter's lair. To the place where the ones with faces are never the same. The ones who can morph their bodies and images to match anyone they have ever seen. Would you dare to walk in their midst knowing that it might be the last time you were ever yourself?

1

I stared through the windshield of my Jeep and saw my target as he approached his black charger. I adjusted the driver's side mirror to get a better look at what was behind me. Never could be too careful with today's society of roughnecks and whatnot.

I stared back at the reflection's eyes, which wanted to bore a hole into my soul. A woman with thick, curly blonde hair with streaks of purple was blowing in the slight breeze that decided to roam throughout my Jeep. I loved having the windows down and the wind blowing my hair at any chance I could get. I normally braided my hair so it was out of my face during work hours, but since today was simply recon, I had decided to let it down. There was a scar on my face that was barely visible, but if you looked hard enough, you could see it in my eyebrow line. It used to be nasty, and I was ashamed to show my face; that day was no longer an issue. I could have easily made the skin smooth again with my shapeshifter powers, but that wouldn't be any fun. I was done with the world telling me what true beauty was. I was a survivor of the past. A past in which I was never going to let myself live again.

I continued watching as my curls swayed, putting me in a memorized state. One moment, I remembered watching my target, and then suddenly, a memory from my childhood flashed before my eyes.

I was six and felt myself running along a field with luscious green grass and wildflowers that tried to cling to my clothes as I raced through the unknown. I loved to watch the cascade of colors from the flowers that changed during every cartwheel. I slowed momentarily and let the subtle breeze blow my curls away from my face. I didn't stay still for long because I giggled, then continued running as fast as possible. One moment, I was upright; the next, I had fallen down during one of my tumbles and hit my face on the hard dirt. I sat there stunned momentarily, but I didn't allow the mistake to slow me down. I got back up and continued cartwheeling, and after every fall, I would always get back up.

"Amy," my Mother called for me.

I stopped what I was doing and forced myself to come back from my own little world. The sky was suddenly dark, and lightning struck the sky. I tried to run to my parents with their arms outstretched, but I never made it in time. The sky opened, and the rain started its downpour.

I quickly blinked back into focus because I only ever had flashbacks when I fell asleep. This time, it was one of the last few memories I held of my childhood before it was ruined by the torture and torment my so-called family held for me. I was a kind soul, yet strong-minded, and this caused my abuser to be very jealous, for she could never break me.

I shifted slightly in the driver's seat of my Jeep and looked at the clock. I had fallen asleep for ten solid minutes. I quickly grabbed the camera from my passenger seat and looked over to where my target had last been seen.

The charger suddenly roared to life, and I began to rapidly snap pictures. I could always delete the ones I wouldn't need later. No sooner did the car roar to life than a woman rushed from the building, holding a large duffel bag with one hand and her chest with the other.

"Let them fall out," I heard the male shout from the car.

"Ha ha! Very funny," the blonde shouted.

She opened the passenger side door, and before she could shut it, the reverse lights shifted to life.

I sighed from the utter boredom that consumed my life at the moment but continued to allow my target to bury himself deeper in his case.

His wife hired me as a private investigator. I worked with a local firm to collect evidence for the divorce courts when needed. I had started this job long before my shifter powers activated in my early twenties.

The money I earned from my dirtier line of work could have easily paid for a lush retirement. I should really think about retiring, but I loved being good at what I did. So, I continued to keep my P.I. license and weapons up to date with state regulations. I continued to work with clients here and there to keep my mind busy and the IRS off my case.

My real job was given through strict instructions via email and then deleted itself upon opening. As soon as a kill contract came my way by email or via safety deposit boxes, I would burn the evidence so nobody could find the details.

I set the camera on the passenger seat, started my Jeep, and began following my target downtown. I stayed at least two lights behind him because, given his reckless driving, he was easy to follow.

Finally, after forty-five minutes, I found his charger sitting outside a crummy overnight place where you paid cash, and nobody asked questions.

"Well baby, we did it!" the blonde shouted from inside the car.

"Shh…" the man said.

I quickly pulled the camera out again because both bodies got out of the car and began to make out on top of it.

"We should take this inside," the blonde said.

"Fine with me," the man said with a gruff voice.

I shut my Jeep off and exited the vehicle with my camera in hand.

"Excuse me!" I shouted to them.

"Huh?" The man said.

"I work for the press, and I was writing a story," I began.

"Get lost, I'm busy," The man replied.

"Fine, I tried to give you a chance," I said as I took several photos of the two of them intertwined.

"What was that for?" the blonde said.

"His wife's divorce lawyer," I said to them as I walked away.

2

When I got back to my apartment, my cat jumped from the top of the refrigerator and into my arms.

"Oh, Beauty," I said as I caught my Russian Blue.

She purred instantly in my arms as I hugged her.

"I hate to say this, Beauty, but for some odd reason, I'm exhausted. I'm going to head to bed early tonight," I told her.

She gave me an unhappy meow but allowed me to set her down on the ground and begin my nightly routine before bed. I didn't have a bad day; just the flashback caught me off guard, and I knew that when I went to sleep tonight, there would be more.

I quickly finished washing my face and brushing my teeth, and then I braided my hair before bed. Beauty gracefully hopped onto the bed and waited for me to get comfortable. I wasn't hungry, so I didn't bother with making dinner. Beauty had her own food bowl if she was hungry.

"It's going to be a rough night," I said as I petted her.

Beauty cuddled up to me, and I quickly drifted into the dream sequences that haunted me.

"She's stubborn but mesmerizing," my Father said.

"That stubbornness will get her in trouble," replied my Mother.

"She has the heart of a lion," my Aunt chimed in. "You two work too hard to have such a child with bad mannerisms and just rude,"

"Nonsense, my children are just fine. They just don't like you, Beatrice," my Father said.

I was hiding behind a wall in the hallway during one of my Aunt's visits.

"You should let me take your children for a while, and you'll see how much they will change. You give them everything they want, " my Aunt paused.

"Whatever gave you the idea that we would allow you to take our children?" my Mother said in a harsh tone.

"Beatrice, leave now and never come back," my Father said with venom in his voice.

My eyes grew wide as I knew family was very important to both of my parents.

The memory quickly changed to one of our neighbors who had become like our family, and we lived a happy life for the time being. They were about to head on a vacation to somewhere out of state, and I wanted to go with them.

"Mom, Dad. Can I go with them?" I blurted out one night.

Both of my parents looked startled.

"I'm sorry, honey, not this time," my Mother said.

"You said that last time!" I screamed out before storming off to my room.

Time blurred again, and the next dream sequence was when the nightmares truly began.

It was Christmas morning, and my sister and I woke up early and rushed to the beautifully lit Christmas tree. My child self thought that we must have been on the good list because presents littered every open space on the living room floor in the basement. I blinked in awe, wondering how we were ever going to get through them all.

Soon, Christmas day was over, and both of my parents were called into work even on the holiday.

"I'm going to have to charge double since it was still the holiday." the babysitter said as she had just rushed into the house.

"That's fine; we were blessed this season with a gracious bonus," my Father said.

Both of my parents left for the day, and unbeknownst to my sister and me, it would be the last time we saw our Mom. Sometime throughout the day, my Father called, noting that he was going to be late, but my Mother was still going to be on time.

Time passed, and it was time for my Mother to come home from work. Except, my Mom never showed up to relieve the babysitter. This was very unlike my Mother not coming home. The sitter decided to turn on the local news. They were talking about a local married woman with two children who had been slain earlier that day.

I had lost my breath because I knew that it was my Mother they were talking about. I couldn't believe it. Nothing bad had ever happened to us before; why would something happen now?

I walked away from both the sitter and my sister and began to sob into the next room. My heart was broken into a million pieces, and I didn't know how to put it back together. My sister must have heard me because she came in with a box of tissues and just allowed me to sob.

My Father quickly came home, and the rest of my family tried to squeeze themselves into our home once they heard the news. Everybody had locked me out of the main living area. I was about to scream, shout, and bang on the door when it opened suddenly.

I walked out to join everyone, and my sister was sitting on somebody's lap. I turned around and went to my room. I sank into myself, and I didn't know how to deal with my grief; I had never felt this pain before.

My eyes welled up with tears as the overwhelming emotions filled me. The tears didn't just threaten to roll over the brim of my eyes; they actually fell upon my soft, young skin.

Inside, I screamed as loud as I could and banged on the internal walls within me. Something stopped me from trying to enter the room where my so-called family and friends were.

After the funeral, my Father tried to do his best with us. Still, we continued to go through the day-to-day motions, not fully functioning without my Mother.

"I will be there for them every step of the way, Beatrice," my Father's voice rang out from an unseen memory.

My Father taught me how to cook, clean, and keep a home functioning. Soon after we were working on the family car, he became very ill. He ended up losing his job and becoming disabled due to the damage to his lungs.

We had to move due to the financial strain. It was hard to see my once invincible Father become something more frail as he continued to worsen. My last memory of him was lying on the couch so he didn't have to go up and down the stairs. My sister and I took care of him the best we could, but it wasn't enough, for he soon succumbed to lung cancer.

My tender heart had broken once more, as I was only twelve when my superhero and best friend had left this world. I couldn't bear the thought of the funeral home, so I wanted to run away.

"Be still, sister," my sister said to me.

I sat still as we were driven in the black funeral limo. Inside the funeral home lay my pale, cold Father. I slowly walked up to the casket with shaking hands and looked inside. I didn't want to be in this world without him, and I wanted to be inside the casket. I had begun to climb inside of the casket to be with my Father. My Aunt Beatrice stopped me, so mentally, I began screaming, crying, and begging them to let me back in with him.

Shortly after the funeral fiasco, we were promised to go live with Aunt Beatrice and Uncle Damien. The hatred that I felt at that moment in time was nothing compared to the hatred I would soon feel for her.

3

The sound of my professional work computer dinging startled me awake. I usually slept with my gun under my pillow, and I pulled it and looked for the danger my body had alerted me to.

After a quick search, I looked around the room. It was still dark out, which meant it was early morning. I glanced at the clock on my nightside table, and it read two in the morning—early like I guessed.

The continuous ringing on my work laptop brought me back to my senses. I rushed over to answer the call when I realized I was wearing shorts and an oversized T-shirt.

"You're late," the male voice said.

I never knew what he looked like, for it was a different person each time, and they were completely blurred and blacked out with a voice disguise.

"I was asleep," I commented.

"You have a new mission; the details will be emailed to you shortly. Memorize it, then leave for the mission right away. This one needs to be taken care of rather quickly,"

"Understood. Is there an additional fee for being handled in a faster manner than usual?" I inquired.

"Yes,"

"Money is always a good incentive to do the job faster,"

"Indeed,"

"Did you at least tell the employer that it will be one month before the target can be taken care of?"

"Yes,"

"I'll leave first thing in the morning,"

"You'll need to drive there,"

"Understood,"

I hung up the call and went to my closet to pull down my suitcases. When I had to drive, I usually packed more clothes and weapons. The ding from my computer sounded again, and I assumed it was the email my employers were talking about.

I quickly went over to read my target's details when the sudden city and state caught my attention. Lebanon, Ohio. I looked over all of the other details and memorized them before the email self deleted.

Great, I was about to head to my hometown, where I had escaped so long ago. I was usually on my own to find a place to hunker down for the time being, but I hoped some of my old haunts would still be in business.

It was late summer and early fall in Ohio, so I packed a mixture of jeans, jackets, shorts, and every article of clothing that I could fit into my suitcase. I also needed to pack my makeup, toothbrush, and anything else that I might need during my trip back home.

For my weapons suitcase, I packed everything that would fit, including some extra ammo in additional cases that looked inconspicuous.

As for Beauty, I would call my pet sitter and have her dropped off at a pet facility that would pamper her and give her the attention she needed. After all, she was quite used to me leaving at all hours of the night and even during the day.

I got dressed for the day in my usual attire for fall weather: a simple t-shirt that didn't show too much, a pair of jeans, and my favorite leather jacket.

I quietly walked out of my apartment with several suitcases in hand and made it down to my Jeep. I wanted to make sure I didn't make any noise, so I made an extra few trips to be sure. I walked back up and gathered more luggage, which I continued for a total of five trips.

With everything packed, I walked back up one more time to leave a note on the counter for my pet sitter and then gave Beauty a treat for being patient with me.

"Goodbye, Beauty. Be good for the sitter," I said out loud.

She meowed back at me in happiness, then returned to her spot on top of the fridge. I grabbed a cold coffee from the fridge and made sure I had my favorite sunglasses in hand as I did my final walkthrough to ensure everything was in its place for when I returned. I had my bills on autopay, so I wouldn't need to worry about anything being paid with a late fee.

Being satisfied with my look, I headed back to the door, walked outside the final time, and locked the door behind me. I checked my watch, and the time read five in the morning. As I walked to my Jeep, there was a figure standing next to it.

I didn't react because I recognized the figure from his outline. He had big beach muscles and sea-licked hair.

"Russell?" I asked cautiously.

"Where do you think you're going?" he asked.

"I already told you that you're not my boss," I said as I continued to walk toward my car.

"I'm your boyfriend." He countered.

"Ex-boyfriend, remember? I broke it off with you. You're too clingy," I said.

"I told you that you can't break up with me," Russell said.

"I'm warning you," I countered.

"Or what?" He said as he pushed himself off of my Jeep.

He reached forward like he was going to strike me when I grabbed his hand and flipped him over top of me. He landed on his back with a loud sound, and the air was being forced from his lungs.

"I didn't know you could do that," he said.

"There's a lot you don't know about me, Russell," I countered.

He rolled over and acted as though he was going to reach for me, and I blocked his advances.

"I see,"

"Leave me alone, or you'll regret it," I replied.

I saw his posture, and he wasn't going to back down.

"Ah crap," I said as I took off my leather jacket and set my coffee and sunglasses on the hood of my Jeep.

He balled both of his hands into fists and was ready to start the fight. I immediately blocked his first punch and struck out with my right leg. He caught it and punched down on my knee, causing me to go to the ground. He laughed maniacally as he leaned over and grabbed my right foot. I tried to scramble away with no use. I rolled over and kicked him with my left foot in the face, causing him to drop my other leg and stagger backward. I got up and quickly kicked him in the stomach and sidestepped out of the way just in time for a backward swing from him. I didn't move out of the way in time as he grabbed my left arm and twisted me down onto the ground. I looked back over my shoulder and saw the menace on his face. I kicked his left leg out from under him, and he began to collapse on top of me. Before he fell completely on top of me, I shoved my foot underneath him and flipped him over top of me, bringing me into the air, and I began to wail on him. Punch after punch until he lost consciousness.

I got up, grabbed my things from the hood of my car, and left him be. I drove off in the direction of Ohio and never looked back to see if he had gotten up from the bloody pulp I left him in.

4

I had driven all morning and finally made it to Lebanon, Ohio. There was an old coffee shop I used to frequent when I was younger, except it was now a bookstore. I looked above the store, and there seemed to be some space. I wondered if it was ready to be lived in.

I walked out of my Jeep, and the autumn chill air hit me in the face like a warm memory. I brushed the sensation off and walked into the bookstore.

"Welcome! Good morning. Please let me know if there is anything that I can help with," the worker greeted me with a warm smile.

"Actually," I started.

"Amy? Amy Dysop, is that you?" the worker greeted me.

"I'm sorry. Do I know you?" I asked.

"You might not recognize me; it has been a few years since high school,"

I cocked my head slightly when the image of a preppy blonde shot into my mind.

"Oh, Brittany?" I asked.

"Yes!" she said as she walked away from the counter.

I could tell she was only a few months pregnant as she was just starting to show.

"Congratulations!" I said to her.

She rushed over to hug me, and I let her embrace me. I hugged her back slightly so she wouldn't think the hug was fake.

"Do you own this place?" I asked.

"No, my Aunt does," Brittany said.

"I remember this used to be a coffee shop. Is the space upstairs still liveable? I mean, is it hopefully ready to be rented by someone?"

"I'm not sure. I know my Aunt had the space available to rent a few months ago,"

"When will your Aunt be back?" I asked.

"She hasn't been back for some time. She has been really sick, and I've been handling the store for her. Let me call her real quick," Brittany responded.

She walked away, flipped out her cell phone, and talked too quickly for me to hear. I walked around the store and noticed a section for local Ohio Authors in the front and several other genres in the back.

"Good news, the space upstairs was just renovated and is ready to move in,"

"How much for a few months?" I asked.

"I'll let you look at the space first to see if you'll like it," Brittany said with concern in her voice.

"I'll take it. As long as it's liveable, it will be fine. I'm only staying for a few months," I countered.

"Here is the price," she said as she wrote the price on a piece of paper.

She slid it over, and I read the numbers, which was a lowball price in today's economy.

"I'll be right back," I said as I exited the store.

I headed back to my Jeep and pulled out my backpack purse with an envelope full of cash. I pulled out the amount that was requested and shoved it into my pocket. I pulled out a couple extra hundred and was going to give it to Brittany as a baby present. Even though I didn't know her, I still loved baby showers.

I walked back inside the store, pulled out the requested money, and handed it to Brittany.

"I know you don't know me anymore, but here is something extra for you," I said as I pulled out the money and handed it over.

"Thank you! I'll put it toward the twins' nursery," she said with tears in her eyes.

"It's no problem, really," I said.

"Let me show you to your new space," she said as she held her belly.

We walked to the back of the store and went up the stairway slowly so Brittany wouldn't lose her breath. There was a door at the top of the stairs, and I was going to guess that this was the room that I was going to be living in for the next couple of months.

Brittany unlocked the door and motioned for me to go first. My initial thought was that the place had been modernized, and the space was bigger than I thought.

"This will do," I said out loud.

"I'm so happy that you like it. The previous renters didn't take any of their furniture, so it's yours now," Brittany smiled.

"There are just a few more things I need to know before I start to unpack the car," I said as I walked around.

"Shoot,"

"Is there another access point to this apartment, or do I need to go through the bookstore every time?"

"Oh, there is a secondary door that leads to the back parking lot with another set of stairs and, of course, the fire escape if necessary," Brittany answered.

"The second thing, where would I find the local motorcycle club? The Rough Horsemen?" I questioned.

Brittany's face went pale at the mention of the motorcycle club.

"You know what you're asking?" she said quietly.

"I do,"

"You can find them at a local pub, but I can't tell you the name. You'll have to find it out for yourself." She said as she began to exit the space.

"Oh, one more thing, Brittany," I said.

"Yes?" she answered with worried eyes.

"Nobody is to know that I'm here," I said.

"Understood," she said quietly.

She held the keys up into the air, and I gently took them from her.

"Are you ok?" I asked.

"The baby's Daddy was part of The Rough Horsemen at one point in time. That was until they abandoned him. That's a story for another time, though," she said.

"Thank you for your discretion," I said as I walked her back toward the main bookstore area.

"Oh! Customers," She said as she hurried off.

I paid her no heed as the smell of books filled me; I would need to purchase a few to keep me occupied as I did my research on my target.

I walked back outside, and again, the air hit me in the face. This truly was my favorite time of the year. I headed over to my Jeep and started it up, and it roared to life from under my touch. I drove to the alley and parked my car in the back parking lot.

"This will be fun," I said to myself as I looked up the stairwell that led to my fully furnished living quarters.

I took several trips and took in the locals who walked the back alleys and paid extra close attention to my vehicle in its parking spot.

5

I had done several recon missions over the last few days trying to get the new lay of the land. Several of my old haunts had closed down, and now there were a crap ton of new restaurants and other local shops that opened in their places.

I decided to sit at an outside Italian restaurant that happened to have several five-star ratings online. Apparently, they served killer food, according to the reviews. Today, I took my time and began on a warm pastry in the morning hours, then decided to nibble on a salad while drinking an iced coffee for lunch. I loved being outside as the air went from cool and crisp to sunny and comfortable.

I had been on my laptop most of the time that I had been here, and the servers even brought a small extension cord to keep my electronics charged. I thought it was a nice touch because I had several personal reports that I needed to complete on my target. When I first sat down, I made sure it was in a shaded spot so my laptop wouldn't have a glare on the screen. I had to admit I was curious as to why an accountant in the middle of Ohio had been a target, so I had reached out to a secluded set of resources that weren't provided by my work associates.

I had been searching hour after hour, and I was about to give up on pulling any type of information on this so-called motorcycle club for which the accountant supposedly did the books. The group was definitely new in town, and I was coming up empty-handed from my own personal searches.

My computer alerted me to an email from one of my outside sources, which was odd because I had expected these results hours before.

Dear Requestor,

We haven't been able to locate any type of information that you requested.

Sorry.

Great, that's just what I needed: an unknown player in the game.

I glanced around with squinted eyes and saw something a bit unexpected. I watched the faces of the unknown shopgoers have nothing but blissfulness and cheer plastered all over them.

My focus began to wane, and I had a hard time not daydreaming about my target again and what he could have possibly done to deserve a hateful ending. From the email that was sent shortly after my meeting, I quickly memorized my target's information. The photo on the docket was of an older-looking man who looked exactly like what an accountant would look like. His name read Stanley Omar. He wore glasses over a middle-aged face with no distinguishing features. The only thing that stuck out from his information was that he did the books for a motorcycle club. I envisioned him being short and more nerdy than a jock.

"Are you finished?" a female server asked.

"No, I'm just nibbling on it," I smiled.

"I understand. Let me know when you're finished," she replied.

Just as I was about to delve deeper into my investigation, the unexpected happened. The bookkeeper, Stanley Omar, appeared at the same restaurant where I was conducting my surveillance.

"Hello, Mr. Omar!" the female server said.

"Hello, Jessica," Stanley greeted her.

I used my laptop monitor and turned the light down so I could see everything from the reflection. He was blushing, and I wanted to almost roll my eyes.

"Are you meeting Mr. Conrad here as well?" Jessica asked.

"Yes! I'm surprised you remembered his name," Stanley said.

"Go ahead and pick a table, and let me know when you and Mr. Conrad are ready to order," Jessica replied.

Stanley nodded and made a move to pull the server, Jessica, closer. She skillfully dodged his advance and headed towards another table. This behavior raised a red flag in my mind. I quickly turned on my laptop camera and began to capture the scene.

Observing him from a distance, I noticed a single man, his hands gripped in nervousness, his eyes darting around in search of his lunch partner. He sat down and looked around him with anxiousness written all over his body language. Once satisfied with his quick look around, he looked over the menu, my guess, to see if they had anything new, and with a look of slight disappointment, he set the menu back down. He pulled his phone out of his pocket, and it looked like he was only partially paying attention to the real world.

The sound of motorcycle pipes crackling nearby caught his attention, and he quickly put his phone away and began to straighten his attire. Three motorcycles were parked just within reach of the outside seating, and all three men entered through the exit gate. *Interesting.*

The leader of the group held up a hand, and two of the men stayed back so they could conduct a little bit of private business. The leader had sat down with the accountant. I watched the two men as they began to head to each table and began to talk to everybody. Once their conversation was completed, the groups would get up and go inside. Before I knew anything, it was my turn for one of the men to come and talk with me. I quickly clicked the recording off just in case he looked at my laptop and was being nosey.

"Excuse me," one of the two men said.

"Yes?" I said as I pretended to look startled and batted my eyelashes at him.

His face turned a slight shade of pink in return, but still, he wasn't deterred from his mission.

"I'm going to need you to leave this area. We have a private business meeting," he said in a low voice.

I looked around, and the other man had already cleared his half of the outside dining area. I was the only one left outside, along with the four men.

"I'm sorry, but my laptop is plugged into the outlet over there, and I really need to get a term paper ready," I said, acting as though I was in college and just working on some homework.

"I'm sorry, but this is private," he countered.

I had a feeling I wasn't going to win this one, so I slowly began to pack up my belongings.

"Alright, if you must have this whole area to yourself," I said jokingly.

The leader of the group got up from this spot and walked over to me, and the other man stepped away. He sat down on the table, and his presence was very ominous. He was used to using his body as a weapon, but so was I.

"Thank you," the leader said.

"You're welcome, Mr.?" I asked.

"You can call me Butch, everybody around here does,"

"Well, Butch, since you must have this space all to yourselves, I guess I must get going," I said, flirting with him.

"Have I seen you before?" Butch questioned.

"Not that I'm aware of?" I purred.

"Let me take you out tonight? To make up for the lost meal,"

"Not tonight; as I said, I have a term paper due. Tomorrow night, on the other hand,"

"Done. Where are you staying?"

"How about I meet you somewhere? Give me your phone," I said as I put my hand out, waiting for him to comply.

He did as I asked and I put my burner number into the contacts. As he got up from the table, he kissed my cheek in a dominance play, and I finished gathering my stuff and left the area.

There was always more than one way to get information.

6

After Butch kissed me on the cheek, there was a slight butter-fly feeling in my stomach. I pushed the feeling aside as I let the clicking noise from my black combat boots hitting the sidewalk fill my entire headspace. I had never caught feelings for a target or their surrounding bodies before, and I wasn't about to let some bad-boy routine catch me off guard. I hadn't realized that I already walked down the back alley toward the apartment door.

I walked up the stairs, and when I opened the door, I half expected my cat to jump into my arms. A slight sad feeling emerged when I remembered that I wasn't in my own home. I sighed but slowly placed my laptop down, and a sudden wave of tiredness washed over me. I was ready for bed even though it was only halfway through the day.

The daylight that had just filled the apartment disappeared in a matter of seconds, and the sky quickly darkened from a luxurious fall day to a severe weather storm. I turned on the TV and flicked over to the local weather station.

"Thanks, Bob. The sky has suddenly gone from a dream to a nightmare. We are advising you to cancel all plans for the evening and stay indoors. This is a severe weather warning, so watch out for torrential downpours and almost flash flooding in certain areas. This is Kathy Shire reporting for the local news," the woman in a pink suit said.

I flicked off the TV and went over to the bedroom to pick out something comfortable to wear to bed. If there was no use going out tonight to get more information, I might as well give in to my sleepy state of mind. After picking out a larger t-shirt and some pajama shorts, I quickly changed and tossed my day clothes onto the floor. I can pick those up tomorrow when I am more focused. I walked over to the bathroom and began my nightly routine of washing off my makeup and brushing my teeth. Once my face was clean, I really looked at myself, my true self.

"You have to," I said to my mirror self.

I tried to focus my mind on Butch's image, and my face contorted in an ugly manner, and then suddenly, my own image was gone. There were Butch's dark eyes that stared back at me. I blinked again, and the face that wasn't my own morphed back to its usual self.

I shuttered because I wasn't normally used to shifting, but I knew I needed to keep my abilities up to par if I was going to keep my career as the uncatchable assassin. I walked out of the bathroom, grabbed my phone off the kitchen counter, and walked back to the bedroom, where I hoped peaceful sleep was going to overcome me. I laid my head down on the pillow and covered up, and no sooner had I closed my eyes than I drifted into sleep.

My Aunt Beatrice's image of her half-dead, decayed body filled my mind; she had been on the shorter side but was very heavy set. She was a monster, someone who dripped venom with every waking step. Her eyes were hollowed out like a skeleton's and a spider web was in the right eye socket.

"Amy!" Beatrice shouted at me, even though I was standing right in front of her.

I was only a child, and I quaked with every word she spat at me.

"Listen to your Aunt, you ungrateful brat!" Damien shouted from down the hall.

He hadn't even been anywhere near us to know anything about the situation.

"The money that you're supposed to be getting will be all mine!" Beatrice cooed.

I looked up at her in defiance, and that was when the sudden searing pain across my face finally registered in my mind. She had struck me for the first time. I looked back at her with shock and put my hand to my face to touch the already sore spot on my cheek.

The sound of the chair at the kitchen table scraped across the floor as my bolstering Uncle got up, undoubtedly to be his wife's sidekick.

"You're nothing but a money-hungry mongrel," I said, staring at her empty eye sockets.

Another radiating pain shot through the same sore cheek, and I knew that she had struck me again. I didn't dare look at her again, afraid that she would get even more angry with the fact that I wasn't going to let her control me. I stared at her hideous clothing, and when my Uncle finally showed up at her side, I stared at his clothes too, trying not to look defiant.

I dared to peek up one more time, and when I did, I saw my Uncle grab ahold of her arm so she couldn't strike me again.

"Stop hitting her. We can't have her all bruised and battered when the adoption agency comes over," he said.

"You're right. We need her to look all fresh and like the little *Princess* her Father always made her out to be."

There was a sudden knock on the door and I prayed for it to be someone to mine and my sister's rescue.

"Don't let anybody see you," Beatrice said as the spider fell from her empty eye socket.

My Uncle hurriedly ran over to the front door to answer it. My Aunt kept me from rushing to whomever had dared to knock at this hour.

"May I help you?" my Uncle's voice echoed throughout the house.

"Excuse me, can Amy come out and play?" a small voice asked.

"I'm sorry, but Amy's not feeling well today; you can come back tomorrow, and we'll see if she's feeling better," my Uncle said with the utmost sincerity as he closed the door.

I guessed he had given my Aunt a look, and she reciprocated it toward me. It was one of pure menace, and she looked like someone who was fighting the urge to strangle somebody.

"Run along, darling; you will need to regain your strength and be better for tomorrow," she said in a silky voice.

I didn't dare say anything or look at her face. Before I could run down the hallway, my Uncle came to the doorway and put his arm around my Aunt. Within seconds, I started to run toward the room that was supposed to be mine and my sisters.

"Not there," my Uncle's menacing voice shouted at me.

I peeked back down and watched as my Aunt and Uncle knew that I had tried to run to the safety of the room that she had supposedly prepared for me. I wanted it to be a sanctuary, but instead, my sister and I had to stay in the attic with all the creepy crawlies and pure darkness.

I glanced into the room, and any type of defiance had left my body as I finished walking down the hall toward the pull-down ladder that would lead up into my worst nightmares.

My sister must have heard everything because before I was able to get to the end of the hallway, the pull-down ladder emerged in front of me. I glanced up the looming stairs and slowly climbed my way into the darkness.

"Hello?" I whispered.

"They're here again," my sister's voice shook.

I rolled over and looked at the clock, and it read just past midnight. I sighed but closed my eyes again and waited for another dream to take over.

I had quickly become the doer of everything within the house. I was responsible for the cooking, cleaning, and anything else that the gruesome couple could think of. My mental health slowly began to diminish at the thought of being in their household forever.

The attic, which I had to call home, was now infested with rats the size of footballs that clung to everything we owned. I would tuck a large blanket around my sister and myself in a cocoon-type fashion to try and hide on the single mattress that we were forced to share. We had one flashlight to share and a bucket for when we needed to do our business. I would often stay up all night secretly reading about other fantasy lives, and I would have killed to escape into their worlds. I remember wishing my Aunt wouldn't have home schooled us so I could tell someone about what she was doing to us.

7

I rolled over, and the bleary room I had fallen asleep in was coming into focus. I sat up and tried to rub the tiredness from my body, but I could still hear the storms that raged outside my windows. I laid back down and tried to go back to sleep.

I had been sleeping when suddenly I heard her monstrous steps pounding against the floor. I glanced out the window in the attic, and it was early in the morning.

"Amy!" she shouted.

I got up as fast as I could and raced down the stairs in my chewed-up pajamas. I didn't dare say anything as I made my way down the stairs. I had just climbed down to the third rung when she suddenly grabbed my arm and yanked me off the rest.

"You ungrateful little beast!" she shouted at me.

"What did I do?"

She didn't say anything else to me as she threw me down the hallway and rushed me toward the basement stairs.

"Please! I don't want to go down there!" I said as she opened the door.

"You'll do as I say," she muttered as she threw me down the squeaky stairs.

I tried to grab ahold of anything that would slow down my fall, but nothing was working, and I floundered around in the emptiness of space and time. I landed on the cold concrete floor of the unfinished basement, and my body hurt from the beating that it had just sustained. I slowly picked up my head and peeked around to see if anybody else was down here, and to my luck, there wasn't.

I heard the crashing noises from upstairs, and then suddenly, the basement door opened again. What I saw truly terrified me. Aunt Beatrice was coming down the stairs with a bowl, and liquid spilled over the sides, making her slip ever so slightly. I tried to move, but the pain from my right shoulder was too much for my fragile body to handle. I glanced back toward my Aunt, and she had finally made it down the stairs, and what I didn't notice was the bottle of dish soap that she also held in a vice-like grip.

"Good, you didn't move. I just got a call from my friend who works with your caseworker. There's going to be a surprise home visit tomorrow, and you need to be spotless for inspection," she said, as she began to scrub my hair and then every being of my clothed body.

Daddy, save me. I cried internally.

The persistent nagging feeling left after every dream that held my past was always in my system the morning after. I looked over at my clock, and I couldn't believe my eyes, it read three o'clock in the afternoon. I sighed heavily but dragged myself to the bathroom before heading into the kitchen.

I was still dressed in my pajamas, but I sauntered over to the coffee pot and set it to the carafe brewing so I could have multiple cups. Soon after, the pot began to fill with the dark liquid, and the succulent aroma began to fill my rented apartment.

I waited patiently for the coffee to finish brewing so I could pour myself a cup into one of the borrowed dishes. Once it was finished, I placed both hands around the mug and pulled it close to my lips before taking a drink, gauging how hot it could possibly be. I allowed for the warmth of the liquid to fill my system, and I exhaled and leaned against the counter with a smile plastered on my face.

I peeked around the room and laid eyes on my laptop. I quickly placed my cup down on the island, grabbed my laptop, opened it, and began to browse the emails that had been sent to me on the previous day.

"Holy cheese and crackers," I said to myself.

I skimmed through at least fifty emails before finally finding something that piqued my interest. The title of the email caught my attention as it was in all capital letters that read FINISH IT. I saw that the email had an attachment, and I was about to click on it to allow the contents to be displayed on my screen when a sudden knock came from the door that led to the outside back alley. I jumped slightly because I hadn't heard anybody walk up the stairs.

I took my time as I went over toward the door to see if the person was truly impatient and just leave with the door unanswered or would wait for me. I waited for just a moment more, then looked through the peephole. I was surprised by the image of Butch being laid back as he waited for me, and there in his hands was a bouquet of flowers.

"Hello?" I called through the closed store.

"Can I come in?" he asked with a smile.

I contemplated on the thought about what he could possibly gain from finding out where I had been staying, since it was supposed to be a secret. After a few short moments, I finally decided what harm could it be, unlocked the doors, and opened them.

"Wow," he said breathlessly as he looked me up and down.

"Can I help you?" I said with a slight smile.

"You're beautiful,"

"I thought our date was for later tonight?" I answered as the butterfly feelings re-emerged.

"Can I come in?" he asked with bedroom eyes.

"Only if you promise not to try and take advantage of me," I answered coyly.

I opened the door for him to enter the apartment, and he whistled as he walked in.

"So this is what the famous Amy Dysop's apartment looks like," he said, a little astounded.

"Not really, it was already furnished before I arrived," I replied, trying to look sheepishly.

He walked into the area as though he had been here before; I quickly walked around him and shut my laptop so he couldn't read what was on it.

"Secretive?" he laughed.

"It's from my work, and if I told you about it, then I'd have to kill you," I said with a smile.

"That's funny. Do you work for the government or something?"

"Or something,"

He had no idea that I was going to frame him for murder in just a short amount of time. I needed this date so I could gather more information about him.

He continued to walk around the apartment and finally settled on the couch. I watched as he moved with fluidity and then sat down as if he owned the place. I had to admit that his bad-boy routine was rather enticing, and I was pondering just how much I truly wanted to get involved in this case.

I went to the fridge, grabbed him a bottle of water, and then grabbed my own cup of coffee, which was starting to cool to room temperature, before I headed toward the living room.

"Water?" I asked.

"Sure, but while I'm thinking about it, why don't we order in?"

"I'm still in my pajamas, and you want to order takeout?" I laughed.

"It is by far the best date attire that I have ever seen," he smiled.

"Fine, what were you thinking?"

"I saw you eating Italian yesterday, so why don't we choose pizza? I'll also have my men drop off some gaming systems, and we can play a racing game,"

"Deal, just no pineapple on the pizza. Also, while we wait for the food, I've got some questions for you,"

"Let me make a few calls," he said as he got up from the couch, walked into the kitchen, and pulled out his phone.

I could still hear his voice as I walked to my bedroom, deciding that I needed to put on some jeans and a bra.

I opened the door, and Butch was standing in the doorway.

"I thought that you weren't going to take advantage of me," I whispered.

He lowered his face down to mine as though he was going to kiss me.

"I can't help it; you make me want to leave it all behind and run away," he whispered back.

"How many times have you used that line before," I said as I began to inch closer.

He didn't answer; he just smiled and began to inch backward ever so slowly.

"About those questions?"

"Only if you let me kiss you,"

"Not on a first date," I said as I backed away and gave us both space.

There was another knock on the door, and Butch hurriedly went over to it as though he already knew who it was.

A s he closed the door, in his hands were both the video gaming system and the pizza.

"There's no way the pizza was done that fast," I chided.

"I already ordered it before I got here. I had a feeling that you were a cheese kind of girl," he replied as he set the pizza on the kitchen island and the system onto the floor.

"That's ok, just make yourself at home," I joked.

The way he acted didn't catch me off guard at all; in fact, the way that he thought I liked cheese was partially right. I did, in fact, like cheese, but also bacon and onions. Where was he getting this information?

"I'll get us the food if you want to hook up the gaming system?" he said out loud as though he was suddenly on edge.

"Why not a movie?" I asked.

"Nah, I think you'll really like the game my guys brought over," he said with a mouthful of pepperoni pizza.

Note to self; Butch really liked to be in control, no matter who it made uneasy. I watched the way he walked with extra close attention to the fluidity in his movements.

"Like something you see?" Butch asked as he wagged his eyebrows.

"Like I said, not on the first date," I replied, trying to make a cool comeback.

I walked over to the kitchen island, grabbed the bag with the video gaming system, and went over to the TV to begin hooking it up. It was super simple: just plug the unit into the wall and one cord into the back of the TV. I did as he asked without too much sarcasm because I wanted to know what he knew. I was already starting to gather some of the details from him, as he was in such close proximity. Thinking of the small details that I had been gathering, I wondered how he knew where everything was.

"How do you know where everything is?" I asked, breaking the silence.

I turned around and caught him staring at my rear end and rolled my eyes in return.

"What? It's basic human nature," he said as he blushed slightly.

"Why Butch, I don't recall you blushing when you kissed me?"

He didn't answer; he just shoved another piece of pizza in his mouth and continued to act as though he hadn't been caught sizing me up. I finished hooking up the system, walked over to him, and closed the proximity between us. There was only inches of space between our hips, and I slowly pushed against him as I reached past him to the cabinet that was directly behind him. Our bodies were pressed ever so slightly together for just a moment, and I could tell that Butch wasn't used to being told no. He was trying with everything in him not to act on his animal instincts and attack me.

"I know what it is that you want to do, getting all hot and sweaty. Making guttural sounds together," I whispered.

"Yeah?" he said breathlessly.

"Let's go to the gym," I said as I pushed myself off of him.

I heard him release a huge sigh as though he couldn't hold back much longer.

"You and I have different ideas about what I want to do," he joked.

I left him, walked to my room, and grabbed my gym bag. I hadn't had any good sparring partners lately and this is a great way to see how he moved in the ring.

I was about to walk out of the room when I heard water running from the kitchen sink. I smiled, knowing that I was driving him crazy and it was going to be his demise. I walked back from the room, and my suspicions were correct.

"I need to grab my bag from the clubhouse before we head to the gym," he said through muffled hands.

"Fine..." I trailed off.

"You ride with me," he said matter-of-factly.

"Sorry?" I said with an accusatory tone.

"There is no way you're going to get me this bothered and walk into the club by yourself,"

"Why? So everybody can think that I'm your property?"

He didn't answer; he just smiled a wide, toothy grin.

"Exactly,"

I sighed, but I allowed him to open the door for me, and he locked it behind him. We both continued to walk down the stairs, with me leading the way.

"Have you ever lived here before?" I asked, calling over my shoulder.

"I guess that one was easy to figure out, huh?"

"Only by the way that you knew where everything was,"

He chuckled, and when we both got to the end of the stairs, he rushed to his motorcycle. He wasn't wearing any type of jacket, and I watched him pull his sleeves up and expose part of his tattoos. I watched as those tattooed arms slowly pulled the motorcycle out of the parked position.

"Where are my manners?" he smiled.

He took his right hand and put two fingers in his mouth, whistled, and the two men who were with him yesterday emerged from around the corner.

"Do you always have an entourage?" I asked.

One of the men came over and grabbed my gym bag, and I handed it over with ease. I didn't need anything in there if I was going to need to fight my way out.

"Of course. You never know when a rival gang or somebody is going to try and take my place. Now, get on," he said while he started his motorcycle.

I walked over to the side of his motorcycle, climbed onto the back, and noticed that there wasn't a bar for me to rest against. He looked over his left shoulder and smiled as though he knew what I was going to say. I decided against it and just leaned forward and hugged him tightly so I wouldn't fall off the back.

"That's a girl," he cooed before taking off down the alley.

I rolled my eyes again, but I knew that he couldn't see me. Once we had maneuvered through the city, it was about a ten-minute ride into the countryside before we were at the supposed clubhouse.

He parked in front of everybody else's bikes, who were already there, as though it was his normal spot. Once he cut the engine, I climbed off the back and shook everything loose.

"Did you have to hit so many bumps?" I asked.

"Yes, just to make you hold on tighter," he replied with a smile.

The two guys that had been in the alley had been following us, and they parked right beside us.

"Make sure she doesn't try to run," he ordered them.

Both of the men got off their motorcycles and began to walk toward me.

"I don't think so," I said as I walked away from both of them and headed inside.

I flung open the door and I saw a bartender serving a hefty crowd, everybody stopped what they were doing and stared. I didn't pay any attention to them and walked up to the bar.

"What will it be?" the male bartender asked.

He wore the patch on his vest that read probate.

"I'll have..." I began.

"A piece of me," a rude biker said.

I sighed and looked at the round man who was truly disgusting.

"You don't want any of this," I said to him as I turned back to the bartender.

The disgusting man slapped me on the rear, and I slowly turned back around, and he made a kissing face at me. He stood taller than I was, but his ponytail swung behind him.

"You really want me to show you a kiss?" I said coyly.

I started to close the distance between us as though I was about to kiss him, and then suddenly grabbed his ponytail and led him away from the bar. The goon squad came rushing over as though to grab me, and I punched goon number one in the jaw, and he dropped to the ground.

"Pathetic," I said out loud.

The dance floor quickly became a sparring arena, and my body ached with adrenaline from needing to use my full potential. The ponytail antagonizer rushed forward as though he was about to grab and try to subdue me, but I saw this move. I dropped to the ground, spun behind the rushing forward motion, and kicked out his knee. He dropped just like I hoped he would. I saw a nearby pool table, grabbed a pool stick, and busted goon number two in the stomach and then the face. Going back to the antagonizer, I pulled the pool stick against his throat and pulled him backward so he couldn't get his footing. I momentarily lost sight of goon number one, and that was when the first strike landed on my back. I dropped one side of the pool stick that I had been holding, and he quickly lunged forward to break away from me. All three men were now in a triangle formation, ready to take me on.

"I'll make you a deal," I said to the one that wanted to kiss me.

"What?" he said, rubbing his throat.

"Let's play for keeps. If I beat you, I get your bike; if you win, you get me," I said.

"What is going on here?" Butch's voice echoed across the room.

"She assaulted me," the biker I had choked answered.

"Cupid, you mean to tell me that you're going to let her win?" Butch responded.

"I want to see what you're made of, Amy," a rogue voice called from the crowd.

Great, now more people know my name.

"Let the fight commence," Butch shouted.

I didn't want everybody to see how well I could really fight. The two goons rushed me from behind and grabbed a hold of me. Cupid came forward and was about to hit me in the stomach when I pushed off the ground and used him as a walking board, causing him to be ushered backward. The running motion caused me to flip over the two goons, and I caused the one on the right to be dragged down with the motion. While the goon on the left was momentarily confused, I rushed over to the goon on the ground, straddled him, and began to wail down with my fist.

Once I was satisfied that he wasn't going anywhere, I knew that my shapeshifter powers were starting to kick in, and I could tell that my strength was more than normal. I grabbed the goon on the left as he looked at me funny, and I could have guessed that my eyes were glowing. It took one punch to the goon, and he was down.

Cupid began to back away from me as I walked toward him.

"I submit!" he shouted.

I felt my rage beginning to simmer slightly, and I wanted more. I looked over toward Butch, and he wore a giant smile on his face.

"Amy Dysop, you surprise me," the phantom voice called out.

The voice that rang out from the crowd continued to catch my attention, but I needed my focus to be on Butch. I needed him to think that I was really interested in him.

"Cupid, sign over your bike first thing in the morning," Butch said as he began to walk down a set of stairs.

I hadn't noticed that he had been in an upstairs area with an over-looking balcony because I was worrying too much about the fight and what I needed to get out of it. My plan on taking Butch to the gym was going to be a little more complicated now.

"So, Glowstick, what's it going to be?" the phantom voice asked.

It was driving me crazy as to why I couldn't remember who the voice had belonged to.

"Glowstick? I like it," Butch's voice rang in the quiet atmosphere.

Cupid scampered away from the middle of the dance floor, and Butch walked over and picked up the pool stick, and began to close the distance between us.

He was within hitting distance, and I had the urge to take him out right then and there. I was already tired of playing a coy little crea-ture that was going to be his property. He wasn't my true target, the accountant was. I needed Butch to be alive so he could be my scapegoat.

He stepped closer and looked into my green eyes, and I looked into his almost black eyes. He used the pool stick and pulled me so close to him that we could have been making love to one another. He leaned down and was about to kiss me when I pulled back.

"Not on the first date," I insisted.

I didn't know for how long I was going to be able to keep this ruse going. I didn't like to entangle myself with anybody that I was going to pin a murder on.

"This is a second date," he said, his eyes shining.

"This is still the first. The sun hasn't set yet," I said into his ear.

He let go of the pool stick and allowed me to step away from him. I took a few steps back, and Butch was right on my heels. I knew that I had him right where I needed him, my little puppet.

I walked back outside, and as soon as Butch followed me, there was a roar inside from his people.

"Get inside!" Butch shouted at the outside stragglers.

I went to his motorcycle and leaned against the seat, and I made my eyes glow slightly.

"Come here," I whispered.

He walked over to me, and I grabbed a hold of his shirt and began to unbutton it slowly, exposing his chest, which was fully tattooed.

"What are you doing?" he asked breathlessly.

"Looking at your tattoos," I said lightheartedly.

"Stop," he said as I got to the last of the buttons before his pants line.

I did as he asked because no means no. There is no greater phrase than somebody asking you to stop. I know what it was like when people didn't listen to me when I begged for mercy.

I pushed him away from me and allowed him to recompose himself. I glanced over toward him, and he was still leaning against his bike.

"So, which one is mine?" I asked.

"What?" he asked barely above a whisper.

"Which one is mine?" I asked again.

Suddenly, my real target arrived at the clubhouse and was very disheveled.

"Butch!" he cried out.

"Stanley? Butch asked, confused.

"Someone is after me," he began. "Somebody just tried to kill me at my apartment in town,"

I turned my head away so he couldn't see my face, but I scowled because that meant there was a double bounty on this guy's head.

"Wait out here," Butch said as he walked back inside.

I didn't say anything but walked away from any light source that would allow for my target to see anything. Once satisfied that I was far enough away, I made sure that my back was turned toward him and started my shift. A shiver ran through my spine as I shed my normal appearance and replaced it with my scapegoat. Even my voice would match his so there wouldn't be any type of discrepancy. The clothes would also match his, so there wouldn't be anything suspicious. I wasn't sure how shapeshifter powers worked, but they have never failed me yet.

"Hey, Stan," I said as I began to walk back toward him.

"How did you?" he began.

"That's not important right now," I said as I closed the distance.

"Someone is out to kill me, and what are you going to do about it?" he shouted.

I put my right foot on a stool that was near him and pulled the knife from my boot that I normally kept at all times. I was about to throw the knife at him and just kill him and be done with it when somebody walked outside.

"Butch?" the phantom voice said.

I looked up, but there was no way this was possible. It was my ex-boyfriend from high school, Jeremy.

I turned toward him and allowed my eyes to glow as much as possible. Jeremy rushed toward me, and I moved just in time. I turned away and released the knife that I had in my hand. I looked over, and Stanley jumped back into his car and drove away.

I shifted back into my usual appearance and glared at Jeremy.

"What are you doing?" I hissed at him.

"I knew it was you as soon as I saw your eyes glowing, and when I saw Butch inside and then him on the camera too," Jeremy cried out. "Nobody put two and two together,"

"Which one is Cupid's bike?" I asked.

"That one, over there," Jeremy said as he pointed to his right.

I couldn't tell the difference between the different types and styles, and there wasn't any light from the day to really look anything over.

"Get me the keys, and I'm gone," I said.

"For how long?" Jeremy asked.

I didn't reply and just waited for him to do as I asked. He left the outside area as Butch came outside and undoubtedly looked for Stanley.

"I want to go home," I said out loud.

"Sorry, Glowstick, you're mine now," Butch said with a level-head-edness that I hadn't seen in him before.

"How many drinks have you had?" I asked.

"What?" he slurred.

"You heard me; how many?"

"It doesn't matter; I own you, remember?"

"I don't recall you owning me. I came out here of my own free will, and I'm going to leave the same way," I said as I began to walk toward him.

"You can't tell me what to do," he said as he tried to slap me.

"Naughty, naughty. Trying to slap a woman," I said as I dodged the oncoming sloppy attack.

I elbowed him in the face, and he bent over to covet his wounds.

I then hit him in the back of the head with my elbow, and he dropped to his stomach and was out.

"Are you serious?" Jeremy's voice called out. "The Rough Horsemen are going to see this as an attack on them and then come after you,"

"Let them,"

"Get out of here," he replied as he tossed the keys in my direction.

10

I grabbed the keys mid-toss, went over to my newly won prize, and started the engine. I found a pair of yellow glasses that usually helped the rider see at night and put them on. I hoped these were Cupid's, too.

"Do you at least remember how to ride?" Jeremy asked tenderly.

"Watch and find out," I replied back.

"You can keep my glasses," he replied.

I peeled out of the parking space and made my way back to town. It was a good thing that when I was eighteen and had been dating Jeremy, he made me learn how to ride and get my motorcycle license, just in case. I took off down the country road with so many flooded emotions that I didn't know what to do. The memories began to flood as I didn't realize I had been taking the same roads that I used to when I was younger and would drive around with no destination. I knew my way back into town but needed the drive to clear my head and the emotions that flooded me.

"Jeremy, I'm scared," I said, holding his hand.

"What are you afraid of? Your Aunt and Uncle aren't here, and you know that I won't let anybody hurt you," Jeremy said.

I looked at his features and saw a baby-faced man with amber eyes and chocolate-brown hair. He could have been a model had his features matured a little bit.

"I have powers," I said, ashamed.

"You have powers? Like magic powers?" he laughed.

"It will be easier if I show you," I paused.

I crunched my nose, closed my eyes, held my breath, and waited for the sensation of my body morphing into another being to take over.

"Nothing is happening," Jeremy said.

I sighed, opened my eyes, and focused on Jeremy's attire for the day. I looked at him really for the first time and wondered what it would be like to have the shape of his face and his entire body. I inhaled slowly and slowed my heart rate, and suddenly, the sensation started. The little tingle in my spine, and when I looked down, I had his hands. I felt my face, and it was Jeremy's.

"Holy cheese and crackers," Jeremy said.

"Holy cheese and crackers," I said, but Jeremy's voice came out.

The mutation didn't stay for long because the tingling in my spine came back, and I was myself again.

"How did you do that?" Jeremy asked.

"I don't know. I haven't told anybody else but you," I whispered.

"Come here," he said, pulling me closer.

We both leaned in, about to kiss.

I blinked back the tears that rolled over my eyes and onto my face and drove faster until it was time for me to merge onto the highway. I had to admit that I was running faster than I should have been, but I made it at least an hour away from Lebanon into a town called Urbana.

It was on the smaller side, and I kept seeing flyers for a flea market on the first of every month. I checked my phone and saw that it was Friday and tomorrow was the supposed flea market. I checked the gas tank at one of the red lights and decided that it was time to get some fuel. I needed something to drink anyway. I was always thirsty after using my powers. Maybe I'll grab one of those jerky sticks, too.

I pulled over to a vacant gas station and headed inside to get my goodies and pay for some gas with my work card so nothing could be traced back to me.

When I walked back outside with my bag, I saw something that I had never thought I would have seen. Russell stood beside my newly won bike, filling up the tank.

"Russell?" I asked.

"Yes?" he answered, as though this wasn't something unusual for him to be doing in the middle of the night.

"What are you doing here?" I said, my annoyance showing.

"I followed you, of course,"

"No, you didn't. How did you find me,"

"Cupid, he's a friend of mine. I was actually in the area, and when he called me saying that my girlfriend with purple and blonde hair was at his clubhouse, I knew that I needed to find you. Also, Cupid has a tracking device on his bike, and he shared the location with me,"

I groaned so loud that I thought I would have woken the sleeping town, but nobody moved from their spots to check on the noise.

"What do you want?" I said as I began to walk again toward the bike.

"You, of course,"

"You think that you can win me back by what? Following me?"

"That's the general idea,"

I didn't want him to know where I had been staying or piece together any information about what I was trying to do in the small town.

"I'm going to be staying here in town for the flea market tomorrow,"

"I can join you. I already know that you're not staying in this town, nor are you going to be here for the flea market. You are staying at an apartment above a bookstore,"

Cheese and crackers, where did he get this information?

My phone began to ring and since I didn't know the number I guessed that it was Butch.

"Hold that thought," I said while holding up one finger. "Hello?"

There was no answer on the other line, and I knew that it was a reminder call from my employers. The charge on the card was probably out of the parameters they had me set, and they were reminding me to get back on task.

"Going somewhere?" Russell asked as he held out an oversized hoodie to me.

I involuntarily shivered but put it on, knowing that I didn't have one for the ride back to the apartment.

"You better not follow me,"

"Of course I will. I'm staying with you," he said, half-cocked.

"I don't think so,"

"Look, you can either let me sleep on the couch, or I'm going to sleep in my car," he replied.

I was done taking orders from men.

"No, you're not. You can stay in your car or go to an overnight hotel or whatever."

I didn't wait for an answer, so I climbed on the bike, which was now full, and took off for the hour back toward Lebanon.

11

When Russell and I arrived back in Lebanon very late, I went straight for the apartment, and he tried to follow me. I parked the bike right next to my Jeep, pulled off his hoodie, and threw it at him.

"Where am I going to park?" he asked.

"Not here," I said as I began to walk up the stairs to my door.

I quickly unlocked the door, shut it, and locked it behind me. I leaned against the door, and I heard the sound of heavy footsteps from Russell, and he tried to catch up to me. The sudden sound of rustling inside the apartment made me look around with my human vision first, and when I didn't see anything, I quickly used my powers and used my night vision.

"Your eyes glow when you do that," Jeremy said.

"Jeremy, I could have seriously hurt you,"

"What are you doing here, Amy? I thought you were never going to come back?"

"One question at a time,"

"Answer me; I deserve at least that much. It better be the truth," Jeremy said with pain filling his words.

"You want the truth?" I asked.

"I already know some of it,"

"Fine, I'm a hired P.I., and sometimes I offer my services to others that are outside my firm," I said, sticking with the truth as much as I could.

"Is that all of it?"

I took a moment to breathe before I answered.

"That's all you need to know,"

"I need to know all of it,"

"No. I can't tell you,"

"How could you use my boss, Butch, to try and kill our accountant?" he asked in a small voice. "Don't think that I don't know that you used your powers when you won that fight earlier today, too,"

"I can't tell you," I said through almost gritted teeth.

"I need to know so I can protect you," he said.

I balled my hands into fists and stalked toward him.

"I don't need you to protect me. I've been doing fine all on my own, making my name known in the private investigator's world. Jeremy, I've got a newsflash. You didn't protect me from my Aunt and Uncle, and you sure haven't protected me over these last few years," I said, knowing this would hurt him.

When I worked up the nerve to look him in the eyes, the hurt I was expecting was there. I knew what I had said, but it didn't make being the person who hurt you feel any better.

"Butch doesn't need to know that we had a past," Jeremy began.

"Will he be here in the morning?" I asked.

"Your guess is as good as mine, but I would say more likely than not, yes,"

"Get out," I said quietly.

Jeremy didn't say anything else as he brushed by me and unlocked the door before heading out.

"Lock the door again," he said.

I was going to do it anyway, but I did lock it back. I leaned against the doorway again and let out a small sigh knowing that

Butch and any other man that I didn't need in my life right now was going to be pounding on the door. I didn't even bother going to the bedroom. I just plopped down on the couch and prayed that there wouldn't be any nightmares tonight.

12

Sleep came easy, and for once, there was no good or bad dream. There was simply nothing but darkness. I awoke to the sound of someone pounding on the door, and I didn't want to get up because I knew that I probably looked horrendous.

"Who is it?" I called out.

"Open the door, Amy," Butch's muffled voice trailed to my ears.

"Open it yourself," I said, still half-asleep.

I suddenly heard the locks starting to turn to the open position, and within moments, Butch and two new goons walked into the room. I grabbed my blanket, pulled it closer toward my face, and put my head back on the pillow I had used all night.

"Awe, isn't the little Glowstick so cute!" Butch cooed.

"Go away," I mumbled.

"Some man outside said that you were his and that you two spent a romantic evening together," Butch said as he grabbed my face.

I grabbed ahold of his hand, twisted it around, and was instantly on my feet. I shoved him against the wall, held him there, and waited for my inhuman strength to kick in. I felt my muscles tense as he tried to push away from the wall but couldn't. It felt joyous as he began to struggle, knowing that he wasn't going to win.

"Glowstick," he purred.

I leaned in close to his ear and waited for his breath to hitch in his throat.

"I'm not your property, and stop calling me Glowstick," I whispered.

I felt his body shiver under my touch, and I let go of him. He pulled on his clothes, including his leather jacket, and unruffled the wrinkles that I had caused.

"Who is the man outside of the apartment?" he questioned.

"Again, what does it matter?" I said as I walked down the hall to the bathroom so I could wash away last night's makeup.

When I opened the door, Butch's face was directly in mine, and it startled me slightly.

"What?" he asked with a slight grin.

"Get out of my way," I said as I brushed past him and headed to my room so I could get ready for the day.

"I don't want to have to ask again..." Butch's voice trailed through the closed door.

His jealousy was starting to get on my nerves, and I wondered what I was going to do now that Russell was in the way. Jeremy was also on my mind; he knew what I really was.

I went to the dresser and changed into a white short-sleeved shirt and a pair of ripped jeans. I grabbed my leather jacket and looked into the mirror so I could quickly rebraid my hair. I blinked just a few times, and my makeup was back in place.

I opened the door, and Butch wasn't standing by the opening, which was a quick relief until I saw him standing near the couch. When I walked closer into the room, I saw all three of my headaches trying to size one up on each other.

"This is a living nightmare," I said as I walked past all three of them.

"Honey, could you please tell them to leave?" Russell asked, slightly intimidated.

"I'm not dealing with this," I said.

I grabbed my phone, keys, and purse and walked out the door, leaving all of them to bicker about anything they wanted to. I heard Butch and Russell's voice yelling at one another. I wanted no part of this; I walked to my Jeep, hopped in, and started the engine. I locked the doors so there wouldn't be any stowaways and headed back toward Urbana. I was bound to have a good day no matter how much fate tried to intervene.

Once I had made it through town, I cracked my windows to let in some of the fall air, and that was when my mood soured. I heard three sets of motorcycle pipes crackling behind me, and I looked in my rearview mirror. Butch waved at me, and I wasn't going to indulge him. I felt my powers surging, and I tried very hard not to break my steering wheel. Butch kept trying to get my attention, but I sped away on the highway, and when I finally got to the town of Urbana, I stopped at another gas station to fill up for the ride back to Lebanon.

All three of the motorcycles had slid in right behind me, and Butch got off of his bike in a hurry. I sighed, knowing that he was going to try to use some sort of swooning act or play the victim.

When he got to where I was pumping gas, he gently placed a hand on my face and began to caress it with the softest of touches. My mind was made up on him and his bad-boy routine. When it came time to complete the job, he was going to rot in prison.

"Sweetheart," he said.

I moved away from his touch, and though it did leave a tingling feeling behind, I still had to keep my head in the game. This feeling was something that I had never felt before. I felt my powers surging again, and I knew that my eyes had been glowing because I could see from the reflection in my windows. It was eerie because you could see the glow behind my sunglasses.

"There's my Glowstick," he said as he pulled his sunglasses off his face.

I watched as his eyes began to glow a dark color, something you would have only seen if you were really looking. I was completely taken aback because I had never met anybody else like me.

"You thought you were the only one?" he whispered into my ear as he pinned me against my Jeep.

Shivers went through my spine because now things just got more complicated.

13

I was about to finish topping off my vehicle when Butch gently pushed me out of the way again. Too many thoughts raced inside my mind. Was Butch a shapeshifter? What was I going to do if he was? I didn't even know what I was until just a few years ago. The powers of a shapeshifter were from my Dad's side, and he had died before he was able to tell me about anything or mention the Ancient Ones.

I felt the urge from deep within my stomach that the Ancient Ones were trying to communicate.

It's time.

From what I was able to understand, each shapeshifter had their own calling. Most of the time, it was for dirtier deeds that needed to be handled within the world. I felt the call from the Ancient Ones when I was twenty, and since then, I haven't disobeyed them. Somehow, they must know that I'm botching this job, and they must be unhappy with how I was handling things. I had never met an Ancient One or even heard of anybody talking about them before. With the knowledge I was able to gather, somehow, they were able to keep track of each and every one of us. That always led to the question of how many of us are out there?

I needed to get some answers but I wasn't sure how the best way was to go about getting them. My original plan of framing Butch wasn't going to fly because there were too many loose strings that could lead back to me. Especially since Russell was here. That also begged the question of what was Butch's role in the Rough Horsemen?

I was about to jump back into my Jeep when something struck me. I turned back around and leaned deep into Butch's ear.

"I've got questions for you, and I need you to ride with me for privacy," I whispered.

I watched as his exposed skin quivered at my words.

"If you wanted alone time, all you had to do was ask," he said. "Park your vehicle, and we'll walk together at the flea market,"

He didn't wait for me to comply as he put the gas cap back and slapped the back of my vehicle. I climbed back inside, started the engine, and headed off into the general direction of the flea market. How did he expect us to talk out in the open with so many prying ears near us?

It had taken me only five minutes to locate the general parking inside the gate. I paid my three dollars to get in and turned off the engines. When I looked around to see if Butch and his entourage were coming in shortly behind me, I was surprised to find only one motorcycle was within the area; when I looked harder, I was only able to see Butch, who was by himself. I couldn't help it, but I shook my head in disbelief. I watched as he didn't even pay to get in. He strolled through and found me standing near my vehicle, waiting for him. He parked right beside me and turned off his ride. I had to admit that it was a rather sexy look.

He walked over and held his arm out as though he was a chivalrous type of man, and I took it like a fool.

"Where is Russell and the other two goons?" I asked.

"Jeremy and my other goon, as you call them, are detaining Russell so you and I can have a peaceful day,"

I blushed slightly but didn't say anything else as we slowly walked to the main attraction area.

"This place isn't as big as I thought?" I said out loud.

"This place holds more knowledge and stories from the past than any other place you will find."

"Have you been here before?"

"It's been a while, but yes, I used to enjoy coming here every month and scouring for any antiques I could find,"

"What changed?"

"I think you know what changed,"

"Speaking of that difficult subject, I need to know more about you and what you are," I whispered.

Butch looked at me with a wicked grin, and he pulled me down a vendor section where there were cars galore. Nobody would think to look at the couple hooking up.

"Like I said, Glowstick, if you wanted time alone, all you had to do was ask."

We were so close that our faces were only inches apart, and my breath was caught in my throat. I was far from being a virgin, but I didn't sleep around with anybody who caught my fancy. Butch bent down and breathed deeply into my ear.

"Why do you smell so good?" he whispered as he nipped at the bare skin of my neck.

"Maybe because we are the same kind," I replied

It took all of my concentration not to give in to him. He continued to trace a line of kisses seductively from the top of my neck down to the bottom. When he was done, he placed his hand on the back of my hairline and pulled hard at my hair.

"Do you know how much control I don't have around you?" he said, his lips almost touching mine.

I turned away from him, showing that I didn't want to go any farther.

"You agreed to answer my questions," I said sheepishly.

"Fine, what is it that you want to know?" he said, pushing himself back slightly off of me.

"The Ancient Ones,"

"What about them?"

"What do you know?"

"Nothing that I am willing to share."

"Fine, are you a shapeshifter like me?"

"Yes, but you are more powerful than I am."

"How do you know?"

"When I tried to push off of the wall, I wasn't kidding when I couldn't do it,"

"What does that mean?"

"It means that your bloodline is stronger than mine when it comes to shapeshifting. How many times can you shift before you can't anymore?"

"I've never tried,"

"I can do ten, and even then, that's a lot. My question is, what are you doing here?"

"The Ancient Ones put me on a darker path, and I'm an assassin,"

"Who is your target?"

"Your accountant,"

"I don't know if I can let you do that,"

He walked away from me and put his hand to his face as though I had just slapped him.

"What do you mean you don't know if you can let me do that? I didn't come here to be part of your possession, but I have a job to do. Let me give you a piece of advice," I said, getting into his face. "There's nothing you can do to stop me,"

I stalked away from him, and when I looked up, to my surprise, I saw my target strolling on his day off.

"Don't!" he shouted.

I looked around and saw that nobody was paying us any attention.

"Fine, have it your way," I said as I began to shift.

I didn't want to do this, but it had to be done. I shifted completely into Butch's appearance, and I saw my reflection in the windows of other cars. My eyes glowed green momentarily, and when I looked back at Butch being the same height as him, there was nothing he could do to stop me.

14

I walked away from Butch and began to go after my prey. Before I was able to take two steps away from him, I felt something hit me in my lower back. When I turned around, I was surprised to see myself standing there.

"Let's even the playing field," I said as I shifted back into my normal self.

Butch's black eyes glowed darker, and I knew my green eyes glowed back.

"This is an unfair fight," my twin said.

"At least it's not going to look like you beat on me."

I looked back to my prey, and he was gone.

The sound of motorcycle pipes crackling caught my attention, and my twin sucker-punched me in the ribs. I dodged out of the way just in time as my twin took a knife from her back and began to slice at me in the air. I continued to dodge until she was close enough for me to knock it out of her hands.

The sounds of the motorcycle pipes crackling caught both of our attention. I completed a full roundhouse kick and caught my twin off guard because the hit landed on her face. She fell to the ground, and I walked over to see if my opponent had been knocked out. Slowly, the body shifted back to Butch's, and I knew that he was truly out cold.

"What did you do?" Jeremy said as he ran to us.

"Jeremy?" I questioned.

"Oh man, this is really bad,"

"What are you doing here?" I snapped at him.

"Come on, we've gotta get out of here, someone called the police,"

I looked around, and to my surprise, the flea market that was bustling with people was suddenly barren.

"Where did everybody go?" I questioned.

"Let's just say that the escapade of you two shapeshifting might have caught everybody's attention," Jeremy said through gritted teeth.

"Here, let me do it before you hurt yourself,"

I walked over to Butch's body and morphed into his stature again; this way, it wasn't so obviously weird with a woman carrying a man out by a fireman's carry.

"You can't," Jeremy stuttered.

I didn't look at him, just hoisted Butch onto my shoulders and began to bypass the vendors, who still gave me a funny look. I felt this pulse beating within me, and I could tell my powers were growing. Oh great. Deep within me, there was this single piece of thread that was so dainty and fragile.

"It would be easier to carry him if you had a wagon," one vendor called out.

"Someone just got overly excited, that's all," Butch's voice came out of my mouth.

"I can't believe you right now," Jeremy whispered as he walked beside Butch's frame.

"What's not to believe?" I asked.

"That you would use your powers for something so evil,"

"You don't understand; it's not like I had a choice in any of this,"

"So you're going to play the victim in this? Sorry, but you don't get to be the evil Queen lopping off people's heads and then crying victim at the end of the day,"

"Alright, I admit that I like playing the evil Queen,"

"Let's just get him back to your Jeep so he can ride his motorcycle back to Lebanon. The sooner you get out of our lives, the better,"

"It's nice to reminisce with you too,"

Both of us had discontinued our conversation, and we stopped right along the gate that would lead to our modes of transportation. I smiled wickedly at him, and he rolled his eyes.

"That would have been more charming if you were actually yourself,"

We finished walking to my Jeep, and I set Butch down on the ground to see if he was going to come too. A sudden idea popped into my head. I went to the passenger side door, opened it, and grabbed a bottle of water. It was still slightly chilled from the overnight coldness that had swept across the area the night before. Without hesitation, I shifted back into myself and walked over toward Butch, who was starting to twitch. I poured the entire contents onto his head and he bolted awake.

"What the?" he yelled as he got up from the wet ground.

He wiped at the droplets that were still on his face and shook his hands toward the ground, trying to get as much water off as he could. He looked around and I saw the confusion written on his face as Jeremy stood beside us.

"Jeremy, explain why you're here," Butch ordered.

"I, uh," Jeremy began.

"Oh, for goodness sake. Jeremy and I used to date back in high school," I cut in.

Butch's eyes had gone wide with the realization that was before him.

"Do you still have feelings for her?" he asked with venom in his voice.

It was uncomfortable to watch Jeremy squirm under his gaze. However, from the nervousness in his body language, it was easy to tell that he did, in fact, still care for me.

"Oh, come on!" I yelled.

Butch didn't say anything, just glared at Jeremy and then at me.

"You have some explaining to do when we get back to the clubhouse," Butch shot at Jeremy.

"I'm done with all of you. First, it's Russell, then Butch, and now Jeremy. I'm not dealing with a love triangle. I came here to do a job, and that's what I'm going to do." I said.

"I still can't let you go through with that plan," Butch said in a low voice.

"You don't own me, even if we are the same species. Besides, I'm running out of time anyway," I replied.

I walked to the driver's side of my Jeep to climb in and was about to start the journey back toward my temporary residency. Butch climbed into the passenger seat before I had a chance to lock the doors.

"Make sure my ride gets back to the clubhouse," Butch told Jeremy.

Jeremy didn't dare say a word; he just nodded his head in agreement.

"As for you…" he began.

"I've had enough of you thinking that you're the boss of me. If you want answers, then we're going to talk this out like normal people," I snapped at him.

He held up one finger as though to try and test me but eventually put it back down and sighed as though he had lost a battle, but not the war. He put on his seatbelt and sat back so I could back out of the parking lot area. Once we had made it out of the small town, I took the back roads the entire way to Lebanon. This way, in case I needed to pull over, it would be easier.

"Talk," I said after twenty-five minutes of silence.

"What do you want to know?" he asked.

"Where do we come from?"

"I'm not sure. I know that I got my calling several years ago from the Ancient Ones. Since then, I have been placed in several towns and different states, starting new branches of the Rough Horsemen. Each town and state has a shifter as its leader. I had to hand-pick each one and ensure that they wouldn't be able to overthrow me in power. You could say that I'm the leader of all of them.

"Why?"

"I don't know, but when you get a call from the Ancient Ones, can you resist it?"

I didn't answer for a moment but thought hard on his words.

"Why do you treat me as your property?" I finally asked.

"I'll tell you the truth, Amy, you are the only female-born shifter I have ever seen,"

That couldn't be right. There had to be others.

"How can that be true?" I questioned.

"I don't know, but I know that I want you as my own," he answered with glowing eyes.

"What if I don't want you in return?"

"Ha! We'll see about that!" he shouted, wagging his eyebrows.

"One last question,"

"What?"

"Why have my powers continued to grow the more I'm around you?"

"It's because your bloodline is the most powerful of all. The more you are around other powerful shifters like myself, the more your powers will grow to prove to me that I'm inferior. It's the natural order of our kind. Think of it like you're a Queen, and I'm a Knight. The more subjects around to control, the more power the Queen gets. The Queen is already powerful on her own, but when she is around more of her kind, she will grow even more so."

That was twice in one afternoon that I had been called a Queen.

15

"**I**'m going to drop you off back at the clubhouse, then head into town so I can go back over my notes and a bunch of other junk," I said authoritatively.

"Or, you could take us back to your place?" he said sleepily.

"Did you actually fall asleep?"

"What can I say? I've never been a peaceful type of man, but being around you puts all of my troubles at ease," he countered.

"I have an idea! If you actually want to court me instead of making snide jokes, why don't you actually put some effort into it?" I said jokingly.

"That's a wonderful idea!"

"I'm kidding,"

"Go ahead with your plan of getting rid of me at the clubhouse. I've got some planning to do," he said, eyes bright.

Great, what did I get myself into?

I stepped on the gas and went slightly over the speed limit. I wanted to get rid of Butch as fast as I could, but I didn't want to get a ticket in the process.

"If you take a right up ahead, it will take you to the clubhouse faster," Butch said sleepily.

I turned on the road that he suggested, and it saved me about ten minutes of drive time. I pulled over and waited for him to get out.

79

"One more thing," he said.

"What?"

He leaned over and kissed me on the cheek and then practically lunged out of the seat. I swatted at him and hid my smile behind a scowl.

"See you later," he waved as he shut the door.

I drove away from the clubhouse and headed back toward town. My stomach growled in protest because of the smells that wafted from the nearby restaurants. I had used too much energy from shifting more times than I was used to. I was also sleepy. I went through the nearest drive-through and ordered three burgers, two large fries, and two large drinks.

I couldn't wait until I got back to the apartment, so I began to devour the food while driving. Not the safest idea, but the smell of the food almost made my stomach churn from the sustenance that I needed for survival. Somebody honked behind me, bringing me from my almost food coma. Good thing I wasn't far from the apartment.

I pulled into the alley and parked my car. I couldn't help but notice that there was only *my* new motorcycle and nobody else's vehicle anywhere nearby.

Thank goodness.

The call for sleep was getting worse by the second. I quickly went up the stairs and unlocked the door, which would allow me some peace for a little while. I quickly shut the door and went to the bedroom so I could get into more comfortable clothes. I didn't care that it was a sunny day and just past lunchtime. I was going to take a much-needed nap. As soon as my head hit the pillows, the dreams started.

"We've been waiting for you," a bellowing male voice sounded.

I got up from the cold table and shivered momentarily, but I looked around the room to see where I was. There was nothing in the vast empty room for me to recognize. *So much for me trying to figure out where I was.*

"Amy, this is not a dream per se," a female voice sounded within the room.

I walked away from the table in which I had been lying on, and when I turned around, it was gone.

"What's going on?" I shouted.

"There is no need to shout," the bellowing male's voice said behind me.

My instincts were on point because they were telling me that somebody was standing right behind me. When I turned around, I saw a man in a dark blue robe with symbols written all over it. I couldn't see his face because it was obscured by darkness from the robe's hood.

"Who are you?" I asked a little quieter.

"We are the Ancient Ones," the female voice said.

I again spun around and saw a female in the same type of robe as the man's, but hers held different symbols and was dark red. The more I looked at the symbols, the more they started to drift off of their clothing. Soon, both figures were standing next to one another. The man was on the taller side, and the woman was close to his height. I still couldn't see the entirety of their faces; the only noises were coming from their moving mouths.

"Why have you failed us?" the female asked.

"I haven't," I replied.

"You didn't kill your mark," the male voice said.

"I was going to do the deed this afternoon until someone stepped in my way," I said somberly.

"You don't understand the severity of this task. If you can't do it, we will send somebody else," the female said.

"Let me ask a question. Why is this man so important to you?"

"He was once an Ancient One and now has gone rogue," the male said.

The female stepped away from the male and began to walk toward me. I didn't want to show her that I was afraid, so I stood very still. She shoved me so hard that I began to freefall from the sky. When I opened my eyes, I was actually falling from the sky, and I didn't know what to do. I had never shifted into an animal before, but I was about to do my best to change into any type of bird that would pop into my mind first. *Falcon.* I shut my eyes really tight, and with every aspect of my body, I willed it to shift into a falcon. As my body did what I commanded it, I was astounded that I had actually morphed into something other than another person. *Open your wings!* I opened my wings and allowed for the freefalling to stop. I allowed my mind and body to adjust to the difference in airflow. There were currents in the sky that I had read about one day from a school report, but one thought continuously ran through my mind. *This was amazing!*

I began to flap my wings to keep myself hoisted into the air, and I rode the currents to the closest town that I could see. I wasn't sure where I was, but hopefully not too far from Lebanon. *What would have happened if I didn't try to morph into an animal?*

The closer I got to the town, the more I realized it was Lebanon. *Thank you, crazy Ancient One, for at least shoving me into reality close to where I was staying.*

You're welcome," the male voice said into my head.

I screeched out in protest at the intrusion into my own mind. *Great, now I'm not even safe in my own mind anymore.* I flew closer to the apartment and I took notice that the sun was starting to set. I couldn't have been gone into the realm of the Ancient Ones for too long because it was just past noon when I had returned for my nap, which I didn't get to take. Another wave of fatigue washed over me, and when I landed on the stairs, I perched for just a few moments as I looked around and saw Butch's bike parked below. If I knew how maybe I would have pooped on it for fun, but being the good sport that I was, I had decided against it. I wasn't sure I was going to be able to do another shift so soon. I hopped over to the door and began to peck on it, hoping that Butch would open it. When he did, he was surprised that I rushed in and flew toward the couch.

"Now, why would a nice birdy like you want to come into a place like this?" he cooed.

I willed my body to morph back into my usual self, and when everything was back in place, I shook momentarily to finish the transformation.

"Surprised?" I asked, feeling drained of all my energy.

"How did you?" he began.

I walked clumsily toward the fridge, grabbed a bottle of water, and began to down it immediately.

"Changing from a bird takes a lot of water…" I said as I had just finished one bottle and grabbed another.

"It's never been heard of for a shifter to be able to use their powers for animals, just other humans,"

"I didn't know that I could do it. One moment, I was laying in bed, and the next, I was somewhere creepy talking to two of the Ancient Ones…"

"You saw the Ancient Ones?" he interrupted.

"Yes, now please let me finish. When the female in the red robe pushed me over, I was freefalling into the air, and something told me internally that I would be alright. I changed into the first bird that I could think of, and then I began to fly back here,"

"You spoke to the Ancient Ones?"

"Yes, keep up,"

"I have never seen or heard anything about the Ancient Ones other than subtle directional clues,"

I stopped drinking my second water and stared at him momentarily. Has anybody else seen an Ancient One?

No.

Thanks a lot for the internal monologue. I desperately needed sleep, but I knew the next thing I was about to do was going to be crazy.

"Butch, I'm really tired. Can I ask you a favor?"

He looked up at me, and for the first time, I saw the real him. The vulnerable person that he tried to keep hidden from the world.

"Name it," he said softly.

"Can we watch a movie, knowing that I'm going to fall asleep? I just don't want to be alone right now,"

"Yes," he whispered.

I walked back to the bedroom to grab my pillow and a huge blanket. I had never felt so exposed, but I didn't want to be alone. Butch had taken off his jacket and made a makeshift footstool out of another piece of furniture. I scampered over to the other end of the couch and began to set up my little nest area.

"I don't think so," he said as he patted next to him.

I was nervous, but I brought my pillow over toward him and set it next to his lap. Then, I began to burrow myself into the blanket before laying down.

"Please, nothing scary," I said meekly.

"Ok,"

He began to rummage through something on one of the archaeological channels, and I was already starting to drift into sleep. He gently placed a hand on the outside part of the blanket where my ribs were, and I was lulled to sleep by the rhythmic petting that he did.

16

I had awoken in the same spot where I had fallen asleep. Butch was still sitting in the same spot on the couch with me wrapped up in my blanket and my huge pillow still in his lap. He was snoring just slightly. I could tell my cheeks burned slightly from a blush that had crept onto my face. *What was I thinking, asking Butch to stay here while I slept?*

"What is bothering that beautiful brain of yours?" he said sleepily.

I didn't say anything; I just pushed myself off of him slightly. He shifted and began to stretch as though he was in some discomfort from his sleeping position.

"I shouldn't have asked you to stay. I don't want you to think that there is more to our peculiar relationship," I said, my voice betraying a hint of uncertainty.

"Relationship?" he laughed.

"You know what I mean. Whatever we have going on here," I said, gesturing between us.

He got up from his seat on the couch and meandered over to the bathroom. I silently judged myself and every action I had taken since the start of this job. This has been one disaster from the next. The door to the bathroom suddenly opened, dragging me from my thoughts, and I didn't wait for him to return to the living room before I headed to the bathroom myself. I passed him in the hallway and made sure that we didn't make eye contact as we brushed past one another. He laughed at my failing attempt to put distance between us. I quickly shut the door, looked into the mirror, and saw my ragged appearance. I had bags under my eyes from the lack of sleep and a drool stain on my face. I couldn't help but feel a pang of embarrassment.

I quickly washed my face and wiped off yesterday's makeup before applying what I would need for the day. My outfit didn't look too rugged, so I decided that I would stay in it.

"Are you going to stay in there all day?" Butch asked.

I walked out of the bathroom and I was able to see that he was rummaging through the kitchen for something.

"What are you looking for?" I asked.

"Ah, so you are going to grace me with your presence. I'm looking for food so I can cook you breakfast,"

I gave him a puzzled look but went to the kitchen area nonetheless.

"I don't have any food," I said.

"I can see that. Then we will have to go out for breakfast,"

"Go out? Your kidding?"

"No. What would be wrong with taking my girlfriend out for breakfast?"

"I'm not your girlfriend,"

"You said we were in a relationship,"

"You know what I meant,"

"I know exactly what you meant, but will I let it slide? Absolutely not,"

I rolled my eyes but went to look for my keys. Not finding them, I began to search everywhere except the one place they actually were. Dangling in Butch's hands.

"Where did you find them?" I asked.

"Right where they were when I got here yesterday. Let me take you out on a real date. What do you have to lose?" he asked with a glimmer of hope in his eyes.

"On one condition,"

"I'm listening,"

"You answer any question that I ask,"

He thought about it for a moment but finally shook his head in agreement.

"What kind of questions do you have that are brimming on the tip of your tongue?"

"I'm not sure yet,"

Without saying another word, we both left the apartment and headed down the flight of stairs to our vehicles. It was a warmer morning for fall, but I didn't know which we would take, his bike or my Jeep. As I waited for Butch to decide, he pocketed my keys and pulled out his own from his jacket.

"Guess you decided to take the bike?" I asked.

He handed me the other helmet, and I put it on, tucking fly-away strands into it. He got onto his bike and waited for me to finish adjusting the helmet before I climbed on behind him. He started to pull away from the apartment, but I wasn't sure where he was going to take us.

Too many thoughts were swirling around my head. What was going to happen to Russel and Jeremy? Did I want this thing between Butch and me to grow into something more? He was the only other shifter that I had ever met, let alone one who knew anything about our kind. There was this undeniable attraction between us. Like I said, there are too many unanswered things.

While I had been lost in my thoughts, I must have instinctually wrapped my arms tighter around Butch because he let go of the handlebars with one hand and touched my hands. I loosened my grip and just buried my head into his back. I didn't want to see where we were going.

Soon, we were turning into a parking lot, and I hadn't realized that a stray tear had escaped and began to make its way down my face. I was so tired of fighting everything and everyone in this wretched world.

You are not alone. Finish your task.

I couldn't even wallow in my own self pity because the Ancient Ones were always butting into my head since yesterday.

17

"We're here," Butch said as he found a parking space.

I looked around, and it was a diner. Butch patted my hands, which were clenched tightly around his chest.

"Sorry," I mumbled.

I got off of the back of the bike first; then Butch followed as he finished parking his vehicle.

"This spot was always one of my favorites. Before I became the leader of the Rough Horsemen, I would always venture over here. They have the best pie," he said.

"Speaking of the Rough Horsemen, why didn't any of them retaliate after I knocked you unconscious at the clubhouse the other night?" I asked.

"Simple. I told them to leave you alone and that you were mine. Some of the men were outraged that I had let you attack me. I explained that I had behaved ungentlemanlike and I deserved every bit of it,"

"You did try to slap me," I said on a more serious note, bringing up the memory.

"Yes. I'm sorry for that. I've never hit a woman before, and I don't plan on starting now. You were literally driving me crazy that night. I knew what you were as soon as your eyes glowed,"

We started to make our way into the diner, and when Butch opened the door for me, it was like walking back in time. The

91

booths were old and worn from use, and some spots on the table were beginning to discolor. There were farmers who were sitting at the bar area drinking their coffee and discussing the oncoming winter, which wasn't far off.

Butch led the way to a secluded booth and immediately sat down. The waitress saw us and walked our way with a couple of menus. Once she reached us, she handed over the menus and advised that she would be back shortly.

I opened mine and tried to decide if I wanted pancakes or an omelet. Butch, on the other hand, hadn't even opened the menu yet.

"I guess you don't need a menu?" I joked.

"I've eaten here enough that I already know what I'm getting,"

"Which is?"

"A surprise omelet. You let the cook decide what to make you,"

"I couldn't do that. I want to know for sure what I'm going to be eating. I'm going to get some pancakes with a side of bacon,"

"Ah, so my lady likes to be in control over her own choices," Butch added with a deadly tone.

"What's that supposed to mean?" I snapped back.

"Nothing, just an observation. That's all,"

Both of us went silent until the waitress came back with a carafe of coffee and poured our helping from the mugs that sat on the table upside down, ready for use when needed. We placed our order and continued in silence.

"Butch, I'm going to be honest. I'm not sure what's going on between us," I said with a blush.

"My dear Amy, is that a blush on your face?" he cooed.

I tried to hide it, but there was no use.

"I'm going to speak my mind. I know that I should be staying away from you. I've never allowed myself to be entangled by people surrounding a case. I'm not sure what has come over me, to be honest. I have so many questions about our kind and where we come from. I just don't know where to start," I blurted out.

Butch sipped the hot coffee from his mug and thought carefully over what I had just said.

"Do you know anything about us?"

"No, my Father died before he could tell me anything. Then my well-being was at the hands of my family; I tried to take care of my sister the best I could," I said in a low voice as a single tear threatened to spill onto my face.

"Amy, look at me,"

I did as he asked and looked him directly in the eyes but didn't say anything.

"Did somebody hurt you?" he asked with venom.

"Let's just say that my life story wasn't the greatest after the death of my parents,"

"What happened?"

The waitress came over, brought our food, and asked if we needed anything else. I quickly wiped away the tears that threatened to ruin my makeup and smiled. She left us alone for the time being.

"I'm not going to get into it. Can you tell me what you know of our kind?"

"Yes. What I know is that a long time ago, when there were castles and whatnots around on the Earth, our kind ruled the land. We actually had our own Kingdom. It was full of traitors from the other Kingdoms that nobody wanted to deal with. You see, every shapeshifter was a man; I'm not sure why, but somehow, throughout history, if a female was born, she didn't survive or something along those lines. The rulers over the Kingdom would always have one daughter, and the rest would be sons. The daughter could see through any disguise or anybody who had shifted into another person's being." he paused while taking a few bites of food.

"The Prince's were just ordinary beings and had the usual shapeshifting powers?" I asked.

"Correct, the Princesses, over the years, began to obtain other abilities and were wanted by all of the other nations. There were many who were kidnapped and forced to marry regular humans in hopes their offspring would produce a more powerful heir. Although the babies would all be normal humans. Typically, after a Kingdom was done with their treasure, they would dump the poor Princess back on the doorstep of her own Kingdom."

"That's terrible,"

"Over the generations, the Princess became more and more powerful, and the Kingdom would automatically ensure she succeeded to the throne to become Queen. When the Queen would have a shapeshifter partner, her children would all be shapeshifters. Again, all boys and one girl to continue the line. After many generations, there was one Princess who was stolen away from our kind and supposedly raised as a human. Many scholars from our shifter lines have tried to trace and find the lost bloodline but have never been successful,"

I tried to process what he was saying. There were ancient bloodlines who held power from our kind. There was only one Princess born every generation. The Queen would always pass down genes for power.

"Wait, I understand that it sounds like I would be that forgotten bloodline, but my mother was ordinary," I insisted.

"Are you sure?"

I looked at him, stared quietly, and continued to eat my pancakes and bacon before they went cold. I finished my breakfast and my coffee and waited for Butch to do the same.

"Any more questions,"

"If I am from the lost bloodline, does that mean I'm a Queen?"

"Exactly. I swear if anybody tries to hurt you, I will put my life on the line for you. Amy, I can't live without you,"

I got up from the table and walked outside for a breath of fresh air.

18

I stood beside Butch's motorcycle and waited for him to finish inside. This was all too much to take in. I was mulling over all of the information that was just given to me, including the part where Butch had just pledged his life over mine. A sudden tingling sensation began to cause a severe itch at the nape of my neck.

I turned around to see what would have caused such a reaction, and to my surprise, my target was standing right behind me. Suddenly, a cloth was over my face, causing me to breathe in the fumes. The world suddenly went dark, and I collapsed.

I opened my eyes to a dungeon-like room, including the manacles that were to hold other prisoners. Looking around the room, I could tell there were torches lit throughout the entire circular room. I squinted to try and see a shadowed part of the area, but my gut was telling me that I wanted nothing to do with anything over there.

A dungeon door opened, and two men walked over in old-time uniforms of pure black and tight against their bodies. Easier for fighting and whatever else these scary looking men did. They undid my manacles, and I dropped to the ground, not realizing how much the chains had been holding me up.

When the two soldiers grabbed ahold of me I felt my power beginning to surge deep within me. *These guys were shapeshifters.* I was trying to find the deep well that housed my power, but I felt like there was something blocking me from it.

I tried not to panic, but I wasn't sure how long I had been hanging on that wall. I couldn't focus on anything other than the soldiers' silent footsteps on the floor. I looked at the brickwork. Was this a castle? Someone opened a door, and there was more light inside this room than I was used to. I squinted in protest.

"Put her there," a voice said.

The two men who had carried me the entire way with ease shoved me into a chair and began to bind me tightly. I didn't look around until I heard the two men had walked out and shut the door behind them.

When I looked up, it was the accountant, but much more lean looking. He was muscled and toned, and he was completely bald instead of balding. His features were no longer of a nerd but of someone who had just walked out of a painting.

"Stanley?" I muttered.

"Ah, so you were able to recognize me. You see, while I'm in disguise, I don't have full access to my powers. Stupid rule about Ancient Ones not having access to their full potential,"

I didn't say anything because I was afraid that I was going to sound stupid.

"Nothing to say? No questions?" he mused.

"I have many questions, I'm not sure where to start,"

"How about, why?" he paused. "Well, go on, ask,"

"Fine. Why?" I asked.

"You see, Amy Dysop. You are the lost bloodline that I've had scholars and others searching to find your family for hundreds of years,"

"I just found out about all of this, so I'm not sure why my bloodline is so important," I scoffed.

"You see, there are a few details that nobody knows. It was your Father's side that gave you the magic you possess in your veins. The Queen so many millennia ago was killed in a war, and she hadn't yet produced any heirs. I was sure that I had ended your bloodline there, yet I didn't have any access to my full potential. I couldn't figure out why until it hit me. The Queen's surviving family must hold the key. The only problem was that they had all gone into hiding before I could get to them,"

I didn't like where this conversation was going, so I tried to fight against the bonds that held me back.

"Oh, you don't like it here?" Stanley asked with a smirk. "You won't be able to break those binds. They were specifically fortified with you in mind. I wasn't sure what type of powers you would have, so I wove a special kind of magic to ward against almost everything. You see, someone from your past was able to melt this with her hands. She could literally call fire to her whenever she felt like it,"

"What do you want with me?"

"What, no other questions? Like, is your sister a shapeshifter, too?"

I knew that my sister didn't obtain any powers, or she would have told me. I stayed silent.

"Oh, so you already know that your Father didn't pass the gene onto her. To be honest I'm not sure how he ended up with two girls instead of the one," he mused more to himself.

There was too much information that had just been presented to me, and I wasn't able to keep up with processing all of it.

"Fine, since you know so much. What do you want with me? To kill me?" I asked.

"That was my initial plan, although the thought of having heirs with the most powerful being on the Earth sounded better. Then, our children would have the ultimate power. Once they would become of age, I would siphon their powers to take for myself," he purred.

"You monster!" I shouted, testing the limit of my binding.

There was no way I was going to let him have his way. I'm not sure what twisted, sick dream he has had, but I wasn't going to be a part of it.

"I'll let you think on my offer,"

19

I fought long and hard against the ropes that seemed to wind tighter the more I struggled. Where was Butch and his unyielding urge to keep me safe?

I was on my own for this one. There was a sudden opening of the only door in the room, and a figure with the same black clothes and a mask showed up.

He rushed over to me and looked me deep in the eyes before he tried to cut the knot with the knife that he had protruded from his back.

"Butch?" I asked.

He didn't say anything, just nodded once as he continued to try and cut the ropes.

"It's no use, these ropes have some kind of magical weave to them. I don't think a regular knife will work," I whispered.

There was a commotion coming from the other side of the door, and then Butch ran out of the room as quietly as he had entered.

Stanley rushed in and began to inspect me as though he knew somebody had just been in here.

"Who tried to help you?" he yelled.

There was too much happening too fast. When Butch put his hand on my shoulder, there weren't any sparks like before. *It wasn't Butch.*

"You think I'd tell you?" I spat at him.

He went behind me and inspected the rope to ensure that I hadn't been able to budge at all. He began to pace the room as though this wasn't supposed to be part of the plan. He suddenly stopped and looked at me with a sinister smile.

"I have a better idea where nobody will find you, my dear," he cooed.

He came over and undid the rope that held me to the chair but quickly tied my hands behind me. He yanked me from my chair and marched me out of the room. There was an attack happening wherever we were.

"This wasn't part of your master plan, was it?

He looked around like a madman as his warriors were beginning to fall to unseen attackers.

"This can't be," he said as he rushed me toward an unseen staircase.

I tried to fight him off, but he was too strong for me. I suddenly felt a pressure in my hands, and I didn't know who it was from; I just grabbed hold of it as though it was the only thing that was going to save my life.

We continued to climb staircase after staircase, going upward in a large circular motion as though he was leading me up to a tower. I needed to think of something fast, or Stanley was going to get his chance to do whatever he wanted with me.

There wasn't a lot of room on the staircase for both of us to fit together, and I began to pull backward with everything that I had. This caught Stanley off guard, but he continued to try and haul me up the remainder of the flights. I struggled against him with every breath I had, and slowly, the rope began to give a little. Although it looked like all my struggling was in vain because we had reached the top of the staircase.

Stanley grabbed ahold of me and shoved me through a small opening in the ceiling, which brought me outside to the raging storm that was wreaking havoc on his castle.

"Where are we?" I shouted into the wind.

"Never mind," he shouted back.

We were at the top of a wide tower and it looked like a sparring area. If you went over the edge, there would be no return. I managed to break free during a blast of wind, and I rushed to the edge, daring to look over. The sudden item in my hands began to simmer to life, and I recognized it as a small blade. I began to cut away my restraint, and by the time Stanley realized what I had done, it was too late.

"Even if you jump, you won't die," he shouted.

The wind let up momentarily, and I could see the swell of power forming around him.

"This place is enchanted against death?"

"No, just yours," he smiled.

He began to maneuver his hands and arms in a way that old-time sorcerers would, and I saw the elements begin to obey his command. *How am I supposed to be all-powerful and not know how to use my powers?*

"I can make you suffer then heal you, time and time again. Unless you come with me willingly," he said as though the magic that he had been holding back was starting to strain against his control.

What was I going to do? There was no place to hide or take cover. I just found out about my shapeshifter powers a few years ago, and I had no clue how to do anything.

You can change into animals. What can't you do?

Thanks, Ancient Ones, for butting in again.

I concentrated on the lighting that was threatening to hit us at every move we made. I allowed the pit of my magic to feel the very energy that it put out, and I held out my hands as though I could wield it.

A sudden burst of pain radiated throughout my being, and I felt on fire. Stanley must have released the magic that he had been containing, and this is what it must have felt like.

I continued to lay on the ground, but the prickling sensation from the lighting was beginning to sting my whole being. Stanley made quick work to recover any distance I had managed to put between us.

When he looked into my eyes, I could see the true menace behind them. I wouldn't let him use me as he wished. He held out his hand as though he was about to pick me up. The lighting that was held deep within me raced from my fingertips as I reached out for his hand.

He tried to recoil but there was too much raw elemental power that flowed into him. His body began to involuntarily quiver, and I saw him being burned from the inside out.

After he stopped convulsing, I looked over and saw his dead eyes that stared back at me. There was too much magic that had flowed into my body too soon. The attack from Stanley and the lighting wielding was more than I could handle. I began to convulse on the ground next to the now-dead Stanley.

"Hold old, Amy," someone said.

I didn't look to see who had come to my aid, but a figure in a dark blue robe stepped out of the shadows.

"How?" I croaked.

"You see, Ancient Ones can't kill one another. After we had heard about what he did, we knew he would retreat to your old family castle, which was hidden away from the world. We sent our hidden warriors to try and rescue you, but you quickly saw that was made a muck,"

"The knife?"

"Ah yes, Katerina had hoped that once you had access to some of your powers, it would work. She was right,"

I laid still while the Ancient One worked on my wounds.

"How bad is it?" I asked.

"It's good that you didn't look. Most of your body is broken, and it will take time to heal,"

"How could one blast take me out so easily?"

"Stanley had mastered so much ancient magic that he was able to combine more than one type together. There was a reason it was banned so long ago. It's dangerous and reckless,"

"What happens now?" I whispered as a deep sleep was starting to take over.

"Rest and recuperate," he replied.

20

"You said she would be awake by now," Butch's voice echoed off the walls.

"Remember to whom you are speaking with," the male Ancient One replied.

I heard pacing around, and I could tell by the sounds of the boots that it was Butch being impatient.

"Butch?" I whispered.

The sudden pacing stopped, and the sound of him rushing back from the few paces he had taken filled the room. I opened my eyes, and I saw him bend so he could be on both knees to be at eye level.

"I'm here," he whispered as though he was trying not to break his composure.

"Did it all really happen?" I asked.

"I can answer that. My name is Seth, and I'm one of the Ancient Ones who has been guiding you. Yes, everything between you and Stanley really happened,"

"Where am I?"

"You are at a healer's place high somewhere on a mountain," Butch said.

"How did we?"

"Get here?" Seth finished. "I brought the two of you here,"

"What will happen now?" I asked, my voice starting to gain more strength.

"That will be between you two. Although, I can tell you from look-ing into your future that you are the Queen of all shapeshifters, and he will be your King. All of those clubs that you have been forming on our orders will soon be stopping by for their own or-ders from you two. You will need to continue doing what you have been doing. By the looks of it, you will have children together, and one will be a baby girl. The other five will be strong young boys. Shall I continue?"

I blushed from what Seth had just said, but he was an Ancient One, after all. I had to shut Butch's jaw because it dropped open in the middle of the conversation.

"I guess you know all," I said quietly.

"You have been relieved from your dirtier line of work, you are going to need protection. You two will need to work out some de-tails; you were able to defeat the most powerful Ancient One. For that, we are grateful. If you need anything, please don't hesitate to contact us. As for you, Butch, we expect you to uphold that oath you said at the diner a few weeks ago,"

Butch nodded his head as Seth began to walk away from my heal-ing area. In the blink of an eye, he disappeared, and we were left to be on our own.

"This is kind of sudden, but with everything that was just foretold about us, I have to ask you something,"

I looked over at him, and he was scared.

"Amy Dysop, Queen of all the shapeshifters, will you marry me?"

I was taken aback by his question, and I started to breathe heavily.

"Yes," I said, looking into his eyes.

Christine Barker is a Christian, full time Mom, a medical prior authorization specialist, and best friend of a fully supportive husband. Currently living in rural Ohio, her husband and two children help assist in taking care of the animals on their small farm. With her love of the outdoors, she always tries to find new ways to engage her children in playing in the dirt and making memories.

She grew up being told to pursue a career towards cooking, but ventured towards the love of reading anywhere she was able. During the elementary years, there was a section carved out for creative writing, and it was her favorite part of the day. A blank slate was carved each day for her imagination to grow in unexpected ways. When not writing, her favorite pastime is watching her children become more independent and learning new skills.

Charmaine loves to spread the word of our Lord and Savior, Jesus Christ. She is married to a kind and continuous servant of our Lord. She is a Mother and Grandmother and lives on the outskirts of rural Ohio. With loving the outdoors and never afraid of a new adventure, she jumped on the bandwagon of authorship and plans on continuing the stories that she can't write down fast enough.

www.ingramcontent.com/pod-product-compliance
Lightning Source LLC
Chambersburg PA
CBHW071334140726
47996CB00005B/1973